"Please, call m
"I think savin
you that right.

He slashed a cynical grin. "Being your fiancé doesn't count?"

She winced at his taunt. "Oh—I—well…"

He shrugged. "Never mind—what can I do for you—Liv?"

Her gaze darted away from his face, ricocheted off the boathouse then pinged up to the mansion. She blinked several times, her fingers lacing and relacing. "I—first…" She slid her attention back to him, and he sensed the move had taken extreme effort. "I want to apologize for the—the engagement thing."

"Ah, yes." He fought a renewed surge of irritation. "I seem to remember hearing something about that in a few newspapers." He lifted a sardonic eyebrow. "Imagine my glee."

Dear Reader,

I had so much fun with my ENCHANTED BRIDES trilogy, I decided it would be exciting to write a series about three brothers. I envisaged each brother to be tough and successful in his own right, but lonely—whether he realizes it or not. Then I decided to place these men on a mountain of emeralds located on their own private island.

The heirs to the Merit emerald dynasty, Jake, Marc and Zack, are as different as brothers can be. But what they have in common is that they are all gorgeous men—who are each about to meet the one special woman for them.

I hope you enjoy Zack's story, *Accidental Fiancée*. Zack is the Merit family badboy, the mystery man, and he likes it that way. But he's thrust into the national headlines when he saves a senator's daughter from certain death. Now, Olivia has accidentally become his fiancée—and they are forced to hide out on Merit Island to avoid the press. The couple's two weeks together are a tormenting, thrilling, life-changing adventure.... Enjoy the ride!

All my best,

Renee Rozel

P.S. I love to hear from readers so do, please, write to me at P.O. Box 700154, Tulsa, Oklahoma, 74107, USA.

THE MERITS OF MARRIAGE

The Merit brothers—
it takes a special woman to win their hearts.

ACCIDENTAL FIANCÉE

Renee Roszel

THE MERITS OF MARRIAGE

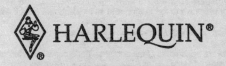

HARLEQUIN®

TORONTO • NEW YORK • LONDON
AMSTERDAM • PARIS • SYDNEY • HAMBURG
STOCKHOLM • ATHENS • TOKYO • MILAN • MADRID
PRAGUE • WARSAW • BUDAPEST • AUCKLAND

To Barbara McMahon and Patti Knoll
for their continued support, humor and friendship
day after day after day after day...

ISBN 0-373-03644-2

Accidental Fiancée

First North American Publication 2001.

Copyright © 2001 by Renee Roszel Wilson.

This edition published by arrangement with Harlequin Books S.A.

Visit us at www.eHarlequin.com

Printed in U.S.A.

CHAPTER ONE

ZACK fell through empty air toward earth. He watched them appear from out of nowhere—the almighty security force that guarded Merit Island. Seconds after he pulled the rip cord on his main parachute, they were no longer scurrying ants, but loomed large enough for him to see the sun glinting off their state-of-the-art artillery.

He grinned. He hadn't expected a marching band to welcome him home after all these years, but he would have preferred to touch down with fewer side arms aimed at his heart.

He attained a zero rate of descent as his feet reached ground level. A perfect landing, especially considering twenty years had passed since he'd seen the topography of Merit Island. His shoe soles skimmed the grass while he sat in his harness. Stepping lightly on the ground, he removed a little of his weight from the rigging. With each successive step he tread more heavily until he fully supported his weight. Coming to an easy halt, he shifted to watch his black-and-silver rectangular chute flutter to the lawn. He also noticed the troops surround him.

As briskly as he could, without making any moves that looked threatening, he took off his helmet and gear, then lifted both hands to reassure the gentlemen in starched gray that he was unarmed and represented no threat, though he was dressed a little like Captain Galaxy in his black jumpsuit.

He smiled at the grim-faced security force as they approached. "Hi, boys," he said with as much friendliness as his desire not to be riddled with bullets could muster. He spread his fingers, his webbed gloves making his surrender look unearthly. Maybe he should have shouted out, "Take me to your leader." He wagged his webbed fingers skyward, surveying the troops. "As you can see, guys…" Making a slow, composed turn, he took a quick inventory of how many muzzles were aimed at his gut.

Eight.

"I can't hide many machine-guns in this sausage-skin getup."

"You'll have to come with us, sir."

Zack glanced at the gray man who'd spoken, no doubt the highest ranking sentry.

"No problem, General." He smiled benignly. "I don't want any unsightly holes drilled in my carcass. Lead the way."

The burly man jerked his head toward the three-story stone-and-timber home Zachary remembered from his childhood. Shifting his gaze from the leader's laser-sighted weapon, Zack stared at the house, his first glimpse since he left home at seventeen. The tightening in his belly surprised him. He'd thought if he ever saw the old homestead again it would seem smaller, somehow less significant. But it didn't.

The image of an English manor house, Zack's boyhood home was still the stately tribute to capitalism it had been all those years ago, with its spectacular view of the Atlantic from the crest of the island's highest point. The sight brought back a wave of feelings, stronger than he'd believed possible. It wasn't the splendor of the residence that made him ache inside, or the memory of the importance of the family dynasty, not the island's primeval beauty or even the vast wealth he'd walked away from all those years ago.

He ached because of the empty hole inside him, a hole that couldn't be filled, no matter how much adventure and excitement he poured in. After a tragic boat racing accident last year when he'd lost his best friend, he'd awakened to the fact of his own mortality, and that a life lived all alone was a barren existence. That realization had sparked the urge to reconnect with family.

Pride had stopped him for much too long. But now that things had gone so royally nuts, he'd been driven by circumstances to come back, pride or no pride. Though the problem that forced him to return to Merit Island made him furious, deep in his soul he was thankful for this chance.

"Sir?" The brawny sentry's guttural prodding jarred Zack to the problem at hand. He peered at the scowling head man, who wagged his weapon in the direction of the house. "Let's go."

Zack nodded, then indicated his chute and rigging. "Would you mind having a couple of your sidekicks gather up my gear, Admiral? Parachutes are bears to repack once they get tangled in a rose garden."

Zack's attempt at a joke died a sober death. Apparently Jake had carried on the family tradition of hiring sentinels who'd had their sense of humor surgically removed. Indicating the mansion with a brisk nod, he offered, "I'm ready if you are, friend."

"My Lord—*Zachary*?"

At the sound of his name, Zack turned, surprised to see his older brother, Jake, appear from the mansion's loggia. He was jogging around the expansive gardens, which, Zack belatedly noticed, were in riotous bloom on this bright, still Sunday in mid-July. Some things never changed.

With a quick grin, Zack shifted to watch his brother's

rapid approach. Ignoring the gaggle of guards, Zack strode toward Jake. "Hey, old man," he shouted, taking off his webbed gloves and tossing them into his discarded helmet. "Don't give yourself a heart attack."

The sentries seemed to grasp that the interloper who'd so outrageously parachuted onto Merit Island might not be there to pilfer from the emerald mine, after all. Stepping back, they allowed him through. Zack noticed firearms being holstered, adding greatly to his capacity for enjoying the afternoon.

Not far behind Jake, several other people appeared, hurrying briskly in his direction. One, Zack could tell, was his younger brother, Marc. Two of the others were women. The wives—Susan and Mimi—no doubt.

A white-haired man emerged from the shadow of the house, and Zack experienced a lurch in his chest. "Well," he muttered, "if it isn't the old tyrant himself."

He didn't have time to contemplate how his father's greeting might go—icy aloofness or heated combat—for at that instant Jake punched his arm in greeting.

"Damn." Jake grinned. "If it isn't the prodigal himself."

Zack was so happy to see his brother, he didn't know how to react. A handshake seemed sterile considering the wealth of emotion he felt.

After a second's hesitation, Jake stepped forward and clasped his brother in a comradely hug. "Blast it, Zack," he said warmly, "It's good to see you."

Zack returned the embrace for a long moment before he could find his voice. "Yeah." It was all he could say and keep his macho image intact. The only day in his life he'd shed a tear had been at his mother's funeral, hating like hell the precious time he'd lost with her by leaving home. Feeling such intense emotion, good or bad, wasn't something he relished, so he swallowed hard, choking back any reaction that might smack of soppiness.

As they separated, Marc, Mimi and Susan arrived. Zack noted that a couple of security guards were gathering up his chute and harness. The others had withdrawn as furtively as they'd arrived.

"Do my eyes deceive me or is it Zachary Merit, the tabloid's hunk du jour?" Marc asked.

Zack eyed his younger brother with high dudgeon. "Very amusing, little brother." He grasped him in a bear hug. "You deal with it for a month, and see how fast you retreat to the old Merit sarcophagus."

When they drew apart, Marc planted his hands on his sibling's shoulders and swept him with a look that Zack could only describe as doctorly. "You've grown into a tall son of a gun," Marc mused aloud, then lifted a hand to Zack's chin, brushing his thumb along to a thin scar that ran from his jaw, across his cleft, ending just short of his lower lip. "Hmm."

Zack knew Marc had become a doctor, but he'd never expected to be the subject of his professional grimace. Though he experienced a twinge at the painful reminder of the freak accident that took his teammate's life, he forced himself to laugh. "How long have I got, Doc?"

Pursing his lips, Marc dropped his hands. "Keep jumping out of planes, buddy, and—"

"Aren't you going to introduce us?"

Zack glanced toward the slender redhead who'd spoken. He winked a brazen "how-do-you-do" and admired the pink color that rose in her cheeks. Susan was exactly as Jake had described, and he understood why his older brother was so crazy about her. "Yeah, Marc," he prodded. "Introductions are in order." His gaze swept from Susan's beautiful blush to the striking blonde who had

taken Marc's arm. So this was the ravishing Mimi. From
everything his brothers had said, Zack decided the married Merit men were damn lucky. He felt a surge of envy,
and was jarred by it.

He eyed Jake, then Marc. "Though you both have
been nauseatingly long-winded about the perfection of
your wives during our phone conversations, could we get
on with the formalities?" He grinned mischievously. "I
have brides to kiss."

As Susan and Mimi were officially introduced to their
brother-in-law, Zack kept track of his father's plodding
approach. He wondered if the old man was intentionally
delaying his arrival to build tension. If that was the case,
it was working. His throat felt parched as he kissed his
sisters-in-law on the cheek.

"They're too good for you bums," Zack kidded, trying
to get his mind off his father's psychological manipula-
tions. "They're beautiful and cultured."

"And pregnant," Mimi added, her cheeks flushing as
she hugged Marc's middle.

Even with his thoughts divided, Mimi's remark came
through loud and clear. Zack gave her his full, apprecia-
tive attention. She wore pink shorts, a white tank top and
strappy sandals, looking trim and fit. He couldn't tell she
was expecting from looking at her. "Oh?" Bowing
slightly in deference, he murmured, "May all your children look like you." He cast Marc a glance and smirked.
"Heaven forbid they should look like the doc."

Mimi giggled. "Now, Zack," she said with a caution-
ing smile, "I think you and Marc bear a striking resem-
blance to each other. Except you have Jake's green
eyes—and those dimples are all yours."

Zack made a playful grimace. "My dear Mrs. Merit,

comparing me to my homely brothers cuts me to the soul."

"All three of you not only look alike, but you share a scary sense of humor," Susan said with a laugh. "And speaking of look-alikes, Zack, you look a little like Darin DeBruin."

Zack glanced her way, going along with her game, whatever it was. "The man is blessed," he kidded. "Who is he?"

Susan's smile grew incredulous. "He's the actor playing you in the movie about you saving Senator Nordstrom's daughter—you know, *Out of the Blue*. Haven't you seen it?"

Zack winced at the reminder. "No, but I might be persuaded to—for a couple million bucks."

"I figured that love story between you and Olivia Nordstrom in the movie was storybook fiction," Jake cut in, "until your engagement was announced in the newspapers yesterday." He drew Susan beneath a protective arm. "I gather the woman's insane, considering she agreed to marry you. But on the upside, our stock jumped five points when the news broke that a Merit was engaged to the future first-daughter of our country. Congratulations, Bro." He extended a hand.

Zack's happy mood sprang a leak and he waved away the handshake. "Take my advice, and sell," he muttered.

"What?"

"Don't mention that woman to me." He dragged a hand through his hair, annoyance overwhelming him for the hundredth time in the past twenty-four hours. "There's no truth to that story. I think your instinct about Olivia Nordstrom being nuts sounds about right."

He watched his brothers and sisters-in-law. Their expressions were priceless. Total confusion. That had been his first reaction, hearing the news, too. The next had been fury.

How the senator's daughter could have told the press they were engaged was too deranged for words. The one time he'd been in the senator's home, he'd been invited for dinner as a "thank-you" for his parachute rescue of their daughter. The whole evening the senator and Mrs. Nordstrom had been extremely cool. He could tell by the look in their eyes that Olivia, their beautiful Yale educated daughter, was off limits to the likes of him—with his reckless lifestyle, racing boats for a living and jumping out of planes for relaxation.

Zack could see by their attitudes they felt he had nothing to recommend him. He had no Ivy League education. For that matter he had practically no formal education at all. Plus, he was sadly lacking in the necessary dancing school manners for acceptance in uptight, conservative circles of their ilk. Oh, he was good enough to save their precious daughter's life now and then, but that was the extent of any relationship he would ever have with her.

Since the ridiculous movie's release last month, he'd grown sick and tired of being unable to go anywhere unmolested by paparazzi or squealing females. As for Olivia Nordstrom's announcement that they were engaged? Clearly the stress of her father's precampaign campaigning, plus the added strain brought on by the movie's popularity, had caused her to suffer some kind of bizarre breakdown.

He'd been traveling home from a speedboat race when the story broke. Stunned, he'd read about his own engagement on the flight. Then, in the wee hours, when he got home, a couple hundred voice mail messages waited for him, demanding that he confirm or deny. The continual ringing of his phone all night had been the final straw.

He was sick of the movie and sick of being linked to the pretty, if a bit too polished and prim, senator's daughter. He wanted his life back, but he had a feeling until this movie stupidity—and now the engagement craziness— died down he wouldn't have any peace.

Slipping out of his high-rise condo at dawn, he'd escaped Los Angeles and made a beeline for Merit Island, off Maine's coast, and its Fort Knox type security.

Though angry with Olivia Nordstrom, he didn't hold grudges and hoped she eventually made a full recovery from her mental collapse. Soon enough the next summer blockbuster, whatever it might be, would draw attention away from the unauthorized movie depicting his rebel lifestyle and the parachute rescue. That day couldn't come too soon for him.

Zack could see that both Mimi and Susan were disappointed to hear the movie's love story was fiction. What romantics his brothers had married. Working to amend the mood of the group, he grinned. "The real Miss Nordstrom is a little tightly wound for my taste," he said. "I like my women—"

"Please don't say loose," Jake broke in. "I'll *pay* you not to say loose."

"Okay, Bro, I'll take that bribe in the form of food. I'm starved." He chuckled, though it was difficult. At long last, his father had joined the circle and was trudging up to front and center.

"How dare you invade our home like some kind of mercenary commando, Zachary?" he bellowed. "I suppose it's *typical* of you. As always—completely self-centered and thoughtless."

George Merit's cutting rebuke brought with it a wave of anguish, evoking memories of their bitter battles. Zack faced the old man. Though his smile felt stiff, he held onto it, determined to make this visit work. He'd promised himself again and again on the trip over that he wouldn't fight with his father. Zack was well aware that he'd been disinherited, and years ago he'd accepted it. He didn't want anything from his family but a little time.

Moving up beside his father, he flung an arm about the older man's shoulders, surprised at how insubstantial he seemed. Zack was three inches taller, at six-five, and outweighed George by fifty pounds of muscle. Odd, he'd always thought of his father an immovable mountain. "It's good to see you, too, Dad," he said, realizing with a jolt that he actually meant it. "What's for dinner?"

Olivia had never expected to see Zachary Merit again after the evening he'd visited her parents' home. The very next day she'd been swept up in the political whirl of her father's quest for his party's presidential candidacy. But this was an emergency. Last week she'd done a stupid thing, and she wanted to apologize in person. Plus, she and Zachary needed to come up with something to tell the press so they would quit dogging her to the edge of insanity. Judging by her half-witted statement, she'd stepped—rather *leaped*—over the edge, at least once.

Frustrated by the tight security that surrounded Merit Island, Olivia ran a hand over her eyes. The outboard and driver she'd hired to take her to Zachary's family home had been stopped by no less than two cabin cruisers, now looming over them like vultures. A dozen warrior-types glared down at her.

"Look, sir," she shouted over the roar of engines, trying to keep the tension out of her voice, "Please tell Zachary Merit that Olivia Nordstrom needs to speak with him in person. It's urgent."

The head scowler spoke into a handheld mike. She

couldn't hear the response, but crossed her fingers, hoping against hope. Zachary must be furious with her for what the papers were saying. She was furious with herself, and mortified that the reporter had taken her sarcastic remark as gospel. But she'd had it up to her eyeballs with stupid questions. That dratted movie and her father's breakneck electioneering pace clearly had gotten to her.

One of the few times in her cloistered life she'd broken out of her Little Miss America mold to do something different, exhilarating, liberating, she would surely have died if not for Zachary Merit's heroism. And how did she repay him? After one too many nosy newshounds demanded ''the truth'' about their relationship, she'd shot back that they were *engaged.*

The humiliating exchange rang in her head so vividly she couldn't keep from running it over and over, like a videotape her traitorous brain was forcing her to memorize in every painful detail.

The journalist, if he could be called that, was a greasy-haired scandalmonger with two nose rings who sold celebrity dirt to the highest bidder. He always wore a baseball cap with Papo emblazoned on the brim, so that's how she referred to him in her recurring murder fantasies.

As usual, he'd been front and center in the crowd, shouting out his questions, interrupting, demanding responses, driving her batty.

''How close is the new film to what actually happened when you were rescued in that parachute accident by Zack Merit?'' he'd yelled.

Ignoring him hadn't worked, so she'd decided she'd better address his questions and get it over. ''In some ways it's quite accurate,'' she said calmly. ''It was a very dramatic rescue.''

''In the film, a romance develops between Olivia and

Zack. I take it that film was accurate in that respect, too?''

''No—that's pure Hollywood fiction.'' She'd wanted to shout, *How many times do I have to deny it? Leave me alone about Zack Merit. Yes, he's handsome, and yes, I'm a female and I was tempted, but he never even looked at me funny. I'm not the type to attract a man like Zachary Merit.* She'd managed to hold on to her smile, but with difficulty.

''Are you sure you want to go on record that it's total fiction?'' he'd prodded with a leer. ''The director insists he researched the rescue very thoroughly—and the people who saw you together said there was definite chemistry between you two. Do you deny that?''

Whatever they might have seen was purely one-sided, her mind screamed. *Zachary Merit was kind, charming and his smile would melt steel, but he was not interested!* ''Er—why—no, there—''

''Why the hesitancy, Miss Nordstrom?'' he'd baited. ''Why not admit it? Something's brewing between the senator's princess and the king of wild abandon?'' He poked his recorder's microphone in her face, but when she only stared, he pulled it back to speak into it. ''Be up-front, Miss Nordstrom. The likelihood of a romance between you two is real, isn't it?''

''I haven't seen Zack lately, so I'd have to say no, probably—''

''And when you *do* see him again?''

The sexual innuendo was embarrassingly clear. Her patience wearing thin, she said, ''Really, this is none of your business.''

''So—you're saying there already has been something between you two, just as the movie suggests?''

Olivia's pounding migraine was beating her down, and

her frustration level had shot to an all-time high. Fed up, she'd retorted, "What do you want me to say? Would it satisfy you if I admit I'm madly in love with my rescuer and we're engaged to be married? Now, *please*, Papo, give me a break!"

She'd said it with such flippancy, she'd been sure the reporter would take it for the sarcasm it was. Who but a headline-hungry member of the paparazzi would take such blatant sarcasm seriously?

After the smoke cleared from her brain, and she read those rash words in print, she'd been horrified. Olivia Nordstrom Engaged To Zachary Merit, the headline shrieked.

Her father, Lawrence Nordstrom, his features an unhealthy shade of purple, had rattled the newspaper over his head, shouting he would commit mayhem before he or any member of his family would be connected with an idle good-for-nothing playboy who—he assured Olivia at the top of his lungs—never voted, never gave a tinker's dam about anything or anyone but himself. Her father's campaign was based on his up-from-poverty-I-am-the-glorious-everyman platform. He hated rich prodigals who lived useless, imprudent lives. Unfortunately that was a perfect description of Zachary Merit.

The senator had demanded that his campaign manager, Jerry Skelton, go "handle" Mr. Merit, for essentially confirming the "revolting" engagement story by his silence. As far as her father was concerned, Zachary was a conniving snake, trying to add luster to his polluted reputation through the senator's cultivated, refined daughter. Olivia would have disagreed if she could have gotten a word in.

First of all, *she'd* been the one to announce their engagement. Second, it certainly hadn't been Zachary's fault, just because he'd been "unavailable for comment" that his silence had fueled speculation. Clearly he'd been out of the country somewhere, and by the time he'd even heard about it, the media hype had escalated beyond repair. His only recourse by then was to avoid the fray. She couldn't blame him. He had to be angry with her. Why should he feel the slightest responsibility to help get her out of her own mess?

Yet, trying to explain that to her father while he fumed and growled and paced was like trying to ward off an attacking bear by pelting it with marshmallows. At least she'd dissuaded him from sending Jerry to sort out Zachary. Jerry's pit-bull personality would only make matters worse. No, it was her fault, she would find the courage to handle it, no matter how angry Zachary might be.

She hated confrontations, but this had to be done, and done by her. Besides, lately Jerry had become bothersomely persistent in his amorous attentions towards her. The senator's delight at the idea of his only daughter marrying Jerry compounded her stress. The flight from her father's California headquarters, where she headed up his finance staff, had been a relief. Not to mention a much needed break from Jerry's possessive—

"Miss?"

Olivia blinked back to a reality filled with intimidating patrol boats and uniformed troopers. She peered up at the head man, her heart shooting to her throat. "Yes?" She wouldn't blame Zachary if he refused to see her, but she had to hope he was more forgiving than her father.

"Mr. Merit said you could come aboard."

"Come—" she was confused "—aboard?"

The man hooked a metal ladder over the side and

stretched out his arm to offer her a hand. ''We'll take you to the island.''

''But...'' She glanced at her driver. ''What about my boat? I hired this man.''

The gray-clad official eyed the boat's muscular young helmsman with a frown. ''I can't authorize the boat, miss. Just you.'' Once again, he held out a hand.

With a reluctant nod, she accepted. ''Okay.'' Turning to the man at the controls of the outboard, she said, ''I'll need you to wait.''

He gave her a narrowed look. '''Fraid not, miss.'' He appeared uncomfortable. In the face of all the hovering muscle, she could understand his misgivings. She wasn't thrilled by the situation, either. ''I'm sure these guys will see you get back to the mainland okay.'' Without making eye contact, he turned away.

Obviously her driver had no intention of staying, so she didn't waste her breath pleading. Working on her nerve, she grasped the ladder and started to climb. Before she reached the top rung, the outboard was buzzing away like a scared gnat, into the setting sun. Olivia's slim skirt and three inch heels made it difficult getting into the cruiser without landing on her head. Dressed more for the boardroom than buccaneering, she had to accept help from two brawny members of the crew.

Ultimately she was welcomed aboard. Well, ''welcomed'' might be a bit of an overstatement. She was hauled on deck without a word, though she noticed a full contingent of speculative looks. It seemed, even out here on the high seas where the Merit Emerald Empire held absolute sway, news of the improbable liaison between herself and Zachary Merit had penetrated the defenses.

During the ten-minute ride to the Merit pier, Olivia sat stiffly on a cushioned bench, fretfully scanning the island that rose and rose before them, out of the sea. A sprawling mansion at the crest of a hill caught her eye, and she stared. It wasn't as though she'd never seen a mansion. Being the daughter of a respected United States senator, she'd been in some swanky homes, but this place...

As daylight faded, the estate's many windows began to glow with golden light. Standing proud and alone, the residence was both compelling and disturbing. The situation seemed surreal, as though she'd been levitated into some crazy kind of alternate universe.

For such an imposing, unbreachable citadel, it almost seemed to welcome her. She breathed in a gulp of sea-laden air, trying to calm her nerves and get her wits about her. *Welcome her, indeed!* What would her reception really be? How would Zachary receive her? With a handshake or a kick in the backside? She swallowed hard, not really believing he'd do her physical harm. Still, he was so—so big. She wasn't exactly tiny, at five-seven. And in three inch heels, she was as tall as lots of men. But Zachary was huge, broad shouldered and muscular.

She experienced a quiver of remembered appreciation. Tall and gorgeous, and compelling and—and disturbing. She quirked a rueful grin. "Like his home," she murmured under her breath. It would have been easy to fall for him—the daring hero who saved her life by risking his own. But he was a thrill-seeker and a lone wolf, no doubt with a half-dozen girls on the string at any one time. Besides, they had nothing in common. It had been better that her parents hustled her off to fourteen-hour workdays of raising campaign funds. It would have been foolhardy of her to harbor silly schoolgirl notions about Zachary Merit.

The boat came to a stop. She bit her lip, apprehensive about what the next few minutes would bring.

"Miss?" The officer in charge offered her a hand. "Mr. Merit is waiting for you."

Her heart performed an unruly two-step as she stood and cast an anxious glance along the dock. When she failed to spot him, she looked at the officer. "Where?"

The man in gray escorted her to the side and helped her onto the pier. "Beyond the boathouse, I believe."

She nodded, stifling the urge to ask, "With a baseball bat?"

Once on the dock, she straightened her skirt and re-adjusted her handbag strap on her shoulder. Clambering on and off cabin cruisers in a slender-fitting linen suit was difficult to do with grace. If Zachary watched her disembark she had to assume he was enjoying a hearty chuckle about now.

Angling her chin high, she marched along the wharf past several other cruisers. Ahead she noted an attractive building, which must have been the boathouse, though it looked more like an oversized cottage, complete with art-ful landscaping, blossoming plants and flowers.

The wooden dock ended and a stone path took its place. Olivia's heart raced as she stepped down onto a walkway that meandered around a corner. Her heart thumping in her ears, she headed into the unknown. Not many steps later, she almost slammed into a towering male blockade in brown shorts and a green polo shirt. Though she'd been warned he was in the vicinity, and had expected him, she shrieked, stumbling a step back-ward.

Pressing her hands to her heart, she tried to breathe, managing strangled little gasps. What was the matter with her? It was only Zachary Merit. He wasn't wielding a bat, and he didn't even look like he'd done any frothing at the mouth.

Lounging against the boathouse, he folded his arms loosely across his broad chest as he surveyed her with shuttered eyes. His silent inspection went on for an interminable couple of pulse beats before one dark eyebrow rose. "Hi, honey," he said, without the hint of a smile. "Have a rough day at the office?"

CHAPTER TWO

OLIVIA'S startled reaction surprised Zack. For a woman who'd jumped out of an airplane, she was pretty nervous about walking around corners. He wondered how she managed to get from her office to her father's without having a full-blown panic attack.

He watched as she gathered her poise. Maybe it was the fiery sunset behind her, but her straight black hair seemed to have a coppery radiance about it. Her skin looked pale. Too pale. Back-lit the way she was, the honey-brown eyes he remembered as huge looked black as pitch. She seemed thinner and looked tired. Maybe it was the dying day throwing him a visual curve. Or maybe Olivia Nordstrom wasn't feeling well. His annoyance abated slightly as he observed her take another shuddery breath.

"Oh..." she presented him with one of the weakest smiles he'd ever seen. "I—you startled me."

He pushed away from the boathouse wall. "Then, I'm glad I changed my mind at the last minute and didn't jump out and shout 'boo.'"

Her smile twitched, but grew no stronger. She was either very tired, very nervous, or both. He slipped his hands into his pockets. "How did you find me?"

She cleared her throat. "Oh—I knew about your family and the island, the emerald business and all, so I took a shot."

"I see." Of course, she would have had no way of knowing he'd been estranged from his family for two decades. A week ago, he would have sworn the likelihood of ever finding him on Merit Island would have been nil. How ironic that he owed his presence here to none other than Olivia Nordstrom, herself. His ire surged, but he hid it. "What can I do for you, Miss Nordstrom?"

"Please, call me Liv," she said. "I think saving my life gives you that right."

He slashed a cynical grin. "Being your fiancé doesn't count?"

She winced at his taunt. "Oh—I—well…"

He shrugged. "Never mind—what can I do for you…Liv?"

Her gaze darted away from his face, ricocheted off the boathouse, then pinged up to the mansion. She blinked several times, her fingers lacing and relacing. "I—first…" She slid her attention back to him, and he sensed the move had taken extreme effort. "I want to apologize for the—the engagement thing."

"Ah, yes." He fought a renewed surge of irritation. "I seem to remember reading something about that in a few newspapers." He lifted a sardonic eyebrow. "Imagine my glee."

She swallowed visibly, thrusting a hand through her glossy hair. Zack bet it felt like silk. The odd thought startled him at first; then he decided it wasn't that odd. After all, Olivia Nordstrom was pretty. A pretty woman, two or three years out of college, from a prominent family. Zack would wager his racing sponsors he wasn't the first male to notice her—and be interested.

But he was no fool. He was thirty-seven, a vagabond who made a fair living at the moment racing boats. In the long run, that didn't mean much to women. They wanted to believe there was more potential for permanence in their men than his lifestyle exhibited—both emotional and physical. What he did was exciting and dangerous, so women seemed to find him exciting and dangerous. And temporary.

Olivia sighed and squeezed her eyes shut. "That remark about our engagement was stupid," she admitted. "I was being flip. That reporter had been driving me nutty with his everlasting inquisition about our relationship, and I just—I just…snapped." She peered at him from beneath her lashes, looking guilt-ridden. "I never—never in a *trillion* years—thought he'd take me seriously. I'm truly sorry." She grasped her skinny handbag strap with both fists. "My father's furious with me."

"I don't doubt it," Zack said. "I'm not exactly the poster boy for ideal son-in-law of conservative presidential hopefuls."

"Hardly," she said, then made a pained face. "Oh—I didn't mean, er…"

He couldn't suppress an ironic chuckle.

She lifted her glance to his face, appearing both surprised and alarmed.

"Don't beat yourself up about it, Liv. My hide's tough. I'm hardly bleeding."

She ran her knuckles across her lips, appearing weary and frustrated. "Zachary," she said. "This isn't how I wanted things to go." She inhaled, looking as though she was working on her resolve. "Could we start over? Why don't you ask me why I'm here?"

He peered at her. "Okay." He didn't know why, but he extended a hand. "Hello, Miss Nordstrom." He paused, and the silence grew deafening.

He could tell when she finally grasped what he was waiting for because she jumped, unclenched a fist from around her handbag strap and slid her fingers into his.

They were cold and trembly. "Hello, Mr. Merit." She sounded more confident than her shaky hand indicated.

His anger slipped a cog, but *only* one. He squeezed her fingers for a second, then released her. "What can I do for you?" he repeated.

This time she managed a smile that didn't look quite so bleak. "According to the Chinese, if you save somebody's life you're responsible for them forever."

Taken off guard by her remark, he said, "But neither of us is Chinese."

She lifted one shoulder and let it fall. "No, but I decided if one of us became angry enough to harbor thoughts of—well—doing away with the other, I might need to remind, uh, the homicidal one of us that he's responsible for me. That means you can't snuff out my lights on a whim."

Her attempt at humor surprised him, and though he had a fleeting urge to smile, he kept his expression skeptical. "Let me see that in the rule book."

Even as Zack made the quip, he had to admit he wasn't as furious with her now as he had been for the past week. In truth, "furious" was a mild word for what he'd felt—having been forced out of *his* town, reporters nipping at his heels.

There was something about the senator's daughter, today, something tangibly vulnerable—in her eyes, her stance and the way she almost-but-not-quite smiled, that made him realize his desire to strangle her had died a quiet death. She didn't look as though she was having the time of her life, either. If he were to be fair, she not only had the bothersome movie and all its ramifications to deal with, she was hip deep in her father's bid for his party's presidential candidacy. That couldn't be a bed of roses.

He was amazed that after being in a bloodthirsty froth for days, he could conjure up sympathy for her. Maybe it was the island's doing—the unending boredom. He wasn't cut out for such a pastoral existence. He was beginning to believe all the quiet was making him lose his will to live—or in Olivia Nordstrom's case—to kill.

"I—I came to ask if you'd be willing to discuss what to say to reporters to get them off our backs once and for all," she said, almost pleaded. "I hoped we might work out a press release we could both live with." Her expression pained and sheepish, she added, "My dad would like us to say we've parted amicably."

Dubious, he asked, "Wouldn't the senator rather have you tell the press you've seen me for the bum I am and dumped me?"

The automatic lighting system for the boathouse and dock clicked on, flooding Olivia with a bright spot. Zack bore witness to the intense blush that crawled up her pale cheeks. He could tell by her sudden, downward glance that her father had suggested exactly that.

"Out of the question," she murmured, then met his eyes. "I would never *dump* the man who saved my life."

He let that statement sink in for a few seconds, and found himself shaking his head at the ridiculousness of the situation, and even more ridiculous conversation. "I'm touched, Liv," he said, only half joking. "I presume you'd like this press release as soon as possible?"

"Yes." She nodded. "I should get right back. But I felt this was so important I had to come myself. It was only fair to you." She managed a slight, embarrassed smile. "Especially since I didn't let you know about our engagement."

"I appreciate being included this time." He indicated the mansion on the hill. "Why don't we go inside where

we can discuss our amicable breakup under fewer spot-
lights.''

Her blush faded somewhat, and Zack noticed, with the
stark light, she really did look unwell. Her eyes seemed
hollow, lusterless. He hadn't seen her for nearly a year,
when he'd had dinner at her home. She'd been attractive
and vivacious, with a golden tan. But this Olivia
Nordstrom was so pallid her beige linen suit seemed dark
by comparison. If he didn't miss his guess, she'd lost
weight. Though she was still lovely, the change wasn't
for the better.

Without determining why, he took her arm. ''It's fast-
est if we cut across the lawn.''

She balked. ''But—across the lawn?''

He halted and glanced at her. ''Is that a problem? Do
you have a grass allergy?''

She shook her head. ''No, but heels don't do well in
grass. They tend to sink.''

''We wouldn't want you making divots in the lawn,''
he quipped offhandedly, glancing at the shoes. Actually
his attention only flicked off the high heels before seek-
ing out slender ankles. ''Take them off,'' he suggested,
working to keep his mind on track.

''And walk in my stockings?''

''That's a problem?'' He met her gaze.

''I'll get a run. I have to wear these stockings all the
way home.''

''I see.'' In fact, he was mystified. She seemed totally
unprepared for this trip. ''What did you think Merit
Island consisted of, a high-rise condo surrounded by
pavement?''

She flushed again. ''I'm afraid my decision to come
was rushed. I—I didn't really think.'' She swept a hand

down to indicate her legs, half exposed below a knee-length skirt.

Those legs had been a major area of interest ever since he'd seen her scramble from the boat, so her insistence that he examine them was criminal. Up until now, he'd made every effort to avoid ogling.

"My plan was to run out here for an hour, then go right back," she said. "I saw no need for a change of clothes."

Deciding he'd given her legs as much attention as was appropriate to the situation, he met her eyes. "Sounds like you had your father's complete approval for this jaunt," he taunted.

She looked away. "Not quite." She glanced back. "He wanted to send Jerry Skelton, his campaign manager, but I didn't think you two would hit it off. Jerry can be…abrasive."

Apparently "abrasive" was the most diplomatic word she could think of. Ol' Jerry must be a real doll. "Were you afraid he'd hurt me," he asked, "…or that I'd hurt him?" He hoped it was the latter, but he had a feeling Liv was protecting him from Jerry's rapier intellect rather than rescuing the campaign manager from Zack's left hook. *So what if she thought of him as a muscle-bound oaf. What in bloody hell did he care?*

She dropped her gaze again, which gave the impression of a coy come-on. *You only wish, Merit!* He squelched the notion. *You're annoyed with her, idiot! Let's not get off track over the way she looks at her own feet!*

"I didn't think you deserved Jerry's barking and growling." He was chagrined to see tears glittering in her eyes. *Damn.* She was having a bad time.

"Jerry might have made some disagreeable remark

about you fueling the rumors by not coming forward to
deny the story. About how you were feathering your own
nest, bolstering your reputation, by allowing people to
think you and I…'' She spread her arms in his general
direction. ''Of course it's ridiculous. I know you were
angry with me, and your silence was your way of telling
me to go to—well, that is—to deal with my own mess,
no matter what Daddy and Jerry might think.'' Hugging
herself, she did that looking-down thing with her lashes
again, and he felt his stomach clench. ''I don't want you
to have any more trouble because of me than—''

''Yeah, thanks,'' he broke in, needing to move, to con-
coct this press release and get her and her sexy-coy eyelashes off the island. Without engaging his thinking processes, he lifted her into his arms. Her gasp didn't
surprise him, and he ignored it.

So her important daddy and his fine-feathered campaign manager thought he was trying to mend his reputation by implying through silence there was a love affair
going on between him and the prim, sophisticated Miss
Nordstrom? As he trudged over the manicured lawn,
holding her in his arms, his annoyance resurfaced. ''Before you announce your next engagement,'' he grumbled,
''either learn to deal with walking on grass or pick on
some guy who doesn't live on such brutal terrain.''

Olivia didn't expect to cross the Merit threshold in
Zachary's arms. If she'd been in a joking mood, she
might have made some reference to the fact that they'd
gone from a quickie engagement to a quickie honey-
moon. But his sarcastic shot about her inability to walk
on grass knocked any idea of joking right out of her,
which was probably for the best. Zachary didn't appear
inclined toward matrimonial banter.

All the way across the sweeping lawn his expression had been one of scowling intensity. His gaze had not met hers once. She knew that because she'd stared at his face the whole way. She had no idea why, but for some reason watching his troubled features, his striking green eyes, his firm mouth, was all she could do.

A muscle knotted in his jaw, and she sensed he'd gritted his teeth. No doubt he was struggling to keep from calling her a silly female hothouse orchid who, not only couldn't walk the distance of a football field on her own two feet, but couldn't get out of a cabin cruiser without the aid of two beefy men.

He already knew she couldn't jump out of an airplane and live to tell about it, unless a man happened to whiz through space, risking his own life, to save her inept backside. What a weak-Wanda impression she'd made on Zachary Merit. Add to that the fact that she'd betrothed herself to him via the newspapers, making him so uncomfortable and angry he'd fled clear across the North American continent! Yes, she was definitely at the top of Zachary Merit's Get-Out-Of-My-Life list.

They entered the mansion through a set of glass-paned double doors, which opened onto a covered patio. Once inside, Olivia was startled to find that she and Zachary weren't alone. Several adults, one toddler and an infant were scattered about a pleasantly furnished den of rich earth tones. Soft music played in the background.

Olivia had a feeling the two women, eyeing her and Zack with strange smiles, had been peeking out, giving a blow-by-blow commentary of their approach. An elderly man with a thick shock of white hair sat on an oriental rug between a marble hearth and a chocolate leather sofa. He cuddled a baby in the crook of one arm. In his free hand, he held a rattle.

When he looked up, his smile faded. His was the only reaction that seemed negative. The other two men grinned openly. A blond toddler, about a year-and-a-half old, sagged sleepily on the lap of another man with green eyes, just like Zack's.

"Well, well, little brother, you left here mad at her and you come back married?" Laying aside a storybook, he winked at Olivia. "If your father is half as persuasive as you, Miss Nordstrom, I predict you'll one day call the White House home." Gently he shifted the drowsy child to the sofa where the little cherub curled up and stuck a finger into his mouth.

"Forgive me." The man with Zack's eyes rose and walked to her. "I should have said *Mrs. Merit.*" He extended a hand. "Welcome to the family."

Zachary cleared his throat and Olivia shot him an apprehensive glance. He didn't look amused, but he did, *finally*, look at her. "Liv, meet our resident comic, Jake, my older brother." Zack nodded toward the man who'd spoken. "Lucky for him, he has a steady job as CEO of Merit Emeralds, because as a comedian he stinks."

Olivia felt herself being lowered to her feet. She did the best she could to land steadily and not make a further fool of herself by toppling over in front of his family.

She shook Jake's hand as firmly as she could. "How do you do, Jake." She hoped somebody would introduce her to the rest of the family before Zack rushed her off to get their business done.

"This is Marc, the baby." Zack indicated another man, lounging against the marble hearth. The pretty blond woman moved to his side and he draped an arm about her.

"The baby?" Marc made a disgruntled face. "Remember, Zack, I'm not above contaminating your orange juice with a flu virus.'' He grinned at Olivia. ''Besides enjoying the questionable honor of being the baby of the family, I'm the resident doctor and this is Mimi, my wife.''

''It's wonderful to meet you, Olivia,'' Mimi said with a smile. ''I guess your leg isn't too badly hurt?''

Olivia was confused at first, then realized what Mimi meant. She shook her head, embarrassed. ''There's nothing wrong. I just—'' She felt ridiculous. ''High heels and lawns don't mix well.''

''I see.'' Mimi's smile widened and she eyed Zack. ''How gallant! We seem to have a regular Sir Walter Ralegh in the family.''

Olivia noted Zack's tan deepen in a flush of unease. With a grunt of what had to be displeasure, he thrust an arm toward the redheaded woman who'd seated herself on the sofa next to the dozing toddler. ''This is Susan, Jake's wife.''

The redhead nodded and smiled. ''It's nice to meet you in person, Olivia. Mimi and I went into Portland the week before last and saw the movie.'' She cast Zack a sly look. ''That's a taboo subject around here, but we loved it. Don't you think Angela Cassio was perfect as you?''

Olivia was embarrassed to be repeatedly compared with Hollywood's latest hot property. ''I haven't seen the movie. It's somewhat of a—'' she bit her lip, trying to come up with phrasing less harsh than her father's ''—a sore point at our house. Daddy was going to sue until he found out Aaron Scott was playing him, and Shellie Shipley was to be my mother—Daddy's loved Ms. Shipley ever since she played that spunky, blue-collar worker in that factory strike movie. He'd never been a fan of Aaron Scott's TV cop show—too wild and disrespectful but Mr. Scott *is* handsome so daddy decided to defer to the movie with benevolent tolerance..." She realized her anxiety was making her babble and she cut herself off, murmuring, "Anyway, I haven't seen it." Desperately wanting to change the subject, she faced the gray-haired man. "And this is your father, Zachary?"

The older man had gone back to rattling the toy over the infant's head. At Olivia's remark, he looked up, his silver eyebrows knitting.

A backdrop of discordant jazz seemed strangely apropos in the conversational rift. Finally, Zack spoke. "Olivia Nordstrom, meet George Merit, our father."

George nodded at her but said nothing, so Olivia merely smiled and nodded back, wondering at the antagonism she sensed between George Merit and his middle son—and evidently anybody he carried into a room. The elder Merit seemed annoyed at her. Of course, he might simply have strong political views that didn't agree with the senator's. She'd run up against that mind-set often enough that it didn't bother her any longer.

"The baby is Benjamin," Zack went on. "Ben's the newest Merit, compliments of Susan and Jake."

"And the sweetheart sleeping on the sofa?" Olivia asked, kneeling to caress Ben's downy head.

"Kyle is our big boy." Susan smoothed the child's hair and glanced at Jake with what Olivia could only describe as adoration. Jake winked at his wife, and even Olivia felt the sensual promise in the act. She swallowed hard and stood, swaying slightly.

She felt light-headed, which wasn't surprising since she hadn't had time to eat all day. Readjusting her handbag strap she returned to Zack's side, certain he wanted to get the press release written. She gave him an "I'm ready whenever you are" look. "We probably should get to work, don't you think?"

"Right." He glanced around at those gathered. "If you'll excuse us, Liv and I have a press release to compose."

"Really?" Mimi asked. "About what?"

"About our amicable breakup," Zack said without smiling.

"Oh?" Susan asked. "That's too bad. I'm sorry to hear you're not going to try to work things out."

Zack stared at Susan, his expression so shocked she might as well have announced that Olivia was pregnant with his child.

After a second, Susan burst out laughing. "Lighten up. I was kidding."

His eyebrows furrowed for an instant before his features returned to some semblance of normal. Even so, Olivia could see irritation in the set of his jaw and the flare of his nostrils.

All of a sudden, he had two noses. How bizarre! She blinked to clear her vision, but it didn't help. Now he had two mouths and two sets of narrowed eyes. She shook her head and tried to refocus, but it only got worse. This time both of Zack's heads spun and the motion made her sick to her stomach.

She felt hot all over—no, cold—no, *clammy*. Raising ponderously heavy hands to her temples, she rubbed. Her fingers were icy. "Zack..." she whispered, "I don't..."

The world went black.

CHAPTER THREE

"YOU did what?" Zack couldn't believe Marc was serious.

"I called Olivia's father and told him she would be here for at least a week."

Stunned, Zack stared at his younger brother. "Why in hell would you do that?"

"She fainted, Zack." Marc clasped his brother on the shoulder. "Being a big celebrity, you may think seeing women faint at your feet is an everyday event, but it's not." He removed his hand, his grin rueful. "I'm a doctor. I went to school to know these things. That woman has worked herself nearly to death. She needs rest and nourishment. I suspect she's anemic. In a week or two I can get her back to normal."

"Can't she get rest and nourishment in California?"

"Apparently she can't, and I don't intend to send her back to the people who ran her down." Marc eyed his brother. "What's your problem with having her here, anyway?"

Zack wasn't sure what his problem was, but he sure had one. "I don't know, she's…" He frowned, shaking his head. "She's…" He had no idea why he didn't want her there. It just seemed like every time she fell into his life, trouble tumbled in with her.

"She's what—beautiful and intelligent?" Marc chuckled. "Yeah, I can see where that might get on a man's nerves."

Unamused, Zack stared at his brother. "That doesn't

36

bother me,'' he said, knowing that wasn't totally true. He had no problem with her good looks, or her brains, for that matter. So what if she was a magna cum whatever from Yale? Who cared if, according to something he'd read, she was a financial wizard—*with soul-stirring eyes and kiss-me lips*? Big deal if he was a hotheaded daredevil with only one real talent—the ability to *drive* anything, from a speedboat to an airplane.

He experienced a stab of distress. Who was he kidding? Maybe his talent had garnered him a degree of fame and money over the years, but she was way out of his league. He'd never even graduated from high school, much of his education collected in the School of Hard Knocks.

Usually his lack of formal education didn't bother him, since he'd done fairly well for himself—the captain of his own ship, so to speak. But Liv Nordstrom was the admiral of a fleet. Around her he felt like a slab of granite—with an absurd case of the hots for a brainy princess who'd taken it upon herself to protect *him* from her daddy's bright-boy bulldozer. He didn't like the feeling.

He exhaled wearily. "And letting her stay here was okay with the senator?"

Marc eyed heaven. "He hated it. But I asked him if he'd rather have his daughter check into a hospital out there, where the press could find out how overworked she was—which I said I'd make sure they did. I hinted the bad publicity would damage his presidential bid. He'd be compared with the slimy Simon Legree character from Uncle Tom's Cabin. What right-thinking citizen would elect a jerk who'd allow his daughter to slave away to the brink of physical collapse? I told him if he really wanted that, I'd bundle her onto the first plane west. But as her attending physician, my recommendation was that she convalesce on Merit Island for at least a week."

"You blackmailed the senator." Zack felt like a volcano on the verge of erupting. He didn't need this!

"Absolutely. I'm not partial to having perfectly fine human beings worked to death—no matter how noble the cause. And for my money, a presidential campaign is not that noble."

Zack had to agree. Though he hated to admit it, Olivia was a whisper of her former self. She hardly weighed a thing, and he should know. He'd spent the majority of their acquaintanceship carrying her around. He peered at the hallway floor, barely noticing the polished wood or the long Persian rug runner. "What did Liv say about it?"

Marc's laugh brought Zack's attention to his face. "I thought I'd let you break the news, since you're such a good friend."

Zack knew why Marc hadn't told Olivia. It was obvious she'd been working hard to help get her father elected, too hard, not eating or sleeping. Nobody could really blame the senator for her condition. He couldn't stand over her with a whip making sure she ate. So, telling Olivia she'd have to take a week off would be a job suitable for only the strongest of men—or the most suicidal. Zack scowled at Marc. "Coward."

"Hey, I blackmailed a senator. Do I have to do everything?" Marc shrugged, his expression going serious. "Besides, Mimi's not feeling well. Her morning sickness comes at all hours, and it's my job to hold a cool cloth on the back of her neck while she's, er, indisposed."

"I'd suggest you get to it, Daddy." Zack indicated Olivia's room. "One last thing, though. Did you remove all sharp objects she might get the urge to throw?"

Marc clapped his brother's arms in a comradely gesture. "You jump out of airplanes, Bro. What can a delicate thing like Olivia do to you? Especially in her weakened condition?"

"We'll find out, won't we?" Zack groused. "I hope you keep a stash of plasma in your office."

Marc turned to go, his chuckle echoing along the hall. "See you in the morning, Lionheart. By the way, Mimi took her some soup earlier." He glanced back and winked. "I figure you deserve a heads-up about the spoon."

Without responding, Zack shifted to glower at Olivia's door. It seemed as though the Fates were conspiring to keep him continually butted up against—er—running into—rather—in close contact— "Damn!" With a determined gnashing of teeth, he headed for her room. The deed was done. She was staying. She might not like it, but there it was.

He rapped on her door, deciding if she didn't answer that would be fine with—

"Yes?"

"Hellfire," he muttered, then called out, "Liv, it's Zack."

"Come in."

He closed his eyes. Why couldn't she be indecent or indisposed or whatever it was women shouted from behind closed doors when they wanted the guy to go jump? He inhaled, deciding he might as well get it over.

The crystal knob turned easily and the door accommodated his slightest touch, swinging open without a squawk. She appeared before him, small and pale in the big antique four-poster with its airy lace canopy. She wore a pale pink negligee—no, it probably wasn't called that, since it was more sweet than sexy. He couldn't see through it and it covered her all the way to her throat. "Hello," he said, then flinched. He didn't sound happy. He worked on upgrading his attitude.

She'd been smiling when the door opened, but her features grew serious. "What's the matter?" She pushed a strand of dark hair behind her ear, appearing anxious. "Do I look that bad?"

He indicated a spindly chair that had been pulled up beside her bed. "Mind if I sit?" He wondered why he'd asked that. Did he plan to stay and chat? *Not on any conscious level, he didn't.*

She glanced at the chair and nodded. "Sure. I was wondering if I'd ever see you again. Everybody else has been by to see how I'm doing—even the baby. Little Ben was more or less asleep, but it was sweet of Susan to suggest he was worried about me." She smiled. "Everybody's been generous and caring." She fluffed the nightgown's ruffled neckline. "Susan loaned me this. She'd bought it for her mother's birthday." Olivia shook her head, seeming overwhelmed. "That's awfully nice. I feel—unworthy of all the fuss."

Zack sat down. The chair creaked and wobbled, but he'd committed himself to sitting, so he sat, hoping the thing wouldn't fall into a pile of antique splinters. He leaned forward to the squeaky accompaniment of straining old wood, and rested his forearms on his thighs. "Marc called your father," he said, seeing no reason to put it off.

She blinked, obviously startled. "Oh?"

Zack nodded. "He told the senator not to expect you back for a week. He said you'll be staying here to relax— and eat. Doctor's orders."

Olivia stared for a long moment, not moving. Zack wasn't sure she was breathing.

"Liv?" he prodded.

She swallowed, making solemn eye contact. "Oh, I couldn't."

"We insist," he assured her, working to sound like he'd had anything to say in the matter. Marc's diagnosis committed her to staying, whether she cared to or not. Besides, Zack didn't like the idea of her passing out at the wheel of her car and careening into a building. He could deal with a week of feeling like a slab of granite. He'd been through worse.

"What did Daddy say?" she asked, her voice fragile.

Zack pursed his lips, choosing to leave out the blackmail part. "He said it was fine."

Olivia continued to stare. Zack thought he saw her swallow again. Just when he was about to call Marc to come and check on what kind of mental collapse was taking place, her eyes began to shimmer. She blinked and a tear skittered down her cheek.

Taken off guard, he sat back. "My Lord! Are you ill?"

She slouched heavily against the pillows that were propped behind her. With a shaky hand, she wiped away the tear. For a long moment she didn't speak or move. She merely stared straight ahead as more tears spilled down her cheeks.

Zack debated whether to take her hand to comfort her or fetch Marc and his medical bag. After a long, baffling minute, Olivia shook her head as though rousing herself from some kind of stupor. Swiping at the moisture on her cheeks, she glanced his way, her pretty lips curving in a tremulous smile. "It seems you're forever saving my life, Zack," she whispered.

Olivia threw back the covers and jumped out of bed. *Enough sleeping and eating.* She wasn't an invalid; she was a perfectly healthy twenty-four-year-old woman! After three days and nights of bed rest, with nothing to do but lie there taking Marc's medicine and eating huge amounts of food, she was mightily sick of herself. She felt like a slug-a-bed, which was the derogatory label her daddy gave anybody who lazed around in the sack after five in the morning.

Luckily Susan and Mimi had anticipated the possibility that one day Olivia would join the land of the living, and had left some clothes. Padding barefoot to the window, she smiled at the bright, sunny day, then went to stand before the closet to scan a rack of dresses, skirts and blouses. Funny, when she thought back she realized she hadn't seen Susan or Mimi in a dress or skirt since she'd been there. Still, they'd deduced she would prefer them. She smiled self-consciously. Was she that predictably conservative?

After a refreshing shower, she slipped into some silky undies they'd left for her. Pristine new. She had a feeling the women had gone shopping on the mainland, just for her. Once again feeling unworthy, she chose a light khaki cotton two-piece with a contrasting band of red at the rounded neck and hem. The waistband was elastic with a drawstring tie. It fit nicely. Not too snug; not too baggy. She hoped Susan and Mimi hadn't bought these dresses, too. Surely not. Underwear she could understand, but not dresses.

She spied a pair of thong sandals and slid her feet into them. They felt strange, flat and flimsy. But she wasn't up to wearing heels; her legs were still wobbly. She blessed the Merit women for their thoughtfulness, and vowed she'd get used to the leather strap between her toes.

A knock at her door made her turn. "Come in."

She was startled to see Zack, since he hadn't been by since that first night. He appeared every bit as startled to find her up and dressed.

She grinned at his expression. He had great eyes. Such a striking emerald color. Right now they were charmingly wide. "Good afternoon, Zachary," she said, feeling suddenly very, very well. He looked fresh and cool in beige chinos and a plaid shirt of muted blues and greens. Why did the sight of this gorgeous hunk, whose discomfort at being around her was painfully obvious, make her light up inside? "You're exactly the man I wanted to see."

She thought she saw the tiniest flinch before he held up a small spiral notebook and pen. "I thought you'd want us to get going on that press release."

She frowned, having completely forgotten about the reason she'd come to the island. With a contemplative nod, she walked toward him. Her last step was a mistake, since something went terribly wrong with her thong or her sapped leg muscles or the cushy carpet. She pitched forward, thudding into Zachary, face first.

"Oof!"

Olivia heard the guttural sound, but wasn't sure if it had issued up from her throat or Zachary's. Both of them had every right to cry out, since both had the breath knocked out of them—Zachary's was due to her head-butt in his stomach, hers to his instinctive grab for her.

She did a little instinctive grabbing herself, and when the haze cleared from her brain, they were clasped together, her nose pressed in the V in his shirt. His mellow aftershave and the warmth of his skin registered strongly.

"If you're too weak to stand up, you should get back into bed."

She canted her head back to look at his face, unsettled

by his coolly patronizing remark. "I'm not the hothouse pansy you think I am. I'm perfectly fine."

"Most people who are perfectly fine can stand alone."

Her feelings bruised, she blurted, "I'm just not used to my *sex*."

"No?" He peered at her and she watched the slow sweep of his long lashes as his gaze narrowed. "I'd think you would be by now."

What was that look? Skepticism. Wry humor? "After I walk in them a while, I'll be okay. I'm just not used to such casual shoes."

His lips twitched strangely, but only for the briefest instant. "Oh, shoes," he said. "You're not used to your *shoes*."

She frowned. "Right. Is that funny?"

He shook his head and released her—almost. Running his hands up her arms, he stepped back as though making sure she wouldn't fall on her face before he let her go. "You said you weren't used to your sex." He pursed his lips and cleared his throat. She had the horrible sensation he was stifling a chuckle.

She bit her lower lip, wondering if that would help staunch the blush creeping up her throat. "I *didn't*," she cried, rejecting the horrible notion. "I didn't—did I?"

He let go of her and broke eye contact, stooping to retrieve the notepad and pen. "Forget it," he said, sticking the items into his pocket. When he faced her, his features were entirely serious. "Why don't I come back after you've had some time to practice walking in sandals, then we can get on with the press release."

Irked by the taunt, she faced him solemnly. "Must you make cracks about everything I do?"

"You can't walk on grass in heels and you can't walk

at all in anything else. What exactly *do* you do, besides fall down?''

That remark cut deep. To keep from showing him how much it hurt, she spun away. ''I'm starved. But don't fret, I bet I'll find the kitchen without a wheelchair and a wilderness guide.'' She stormed toward the door. ''Thanks anyway.''

He didn't answer.

''You're a real prince,'' Zack muttered to himself as he sat alone on the loggia. ''She's just out of her sick bed. She's wobbly, and she stumbles into you and you act like she demanded that you scrub her back! She's not looking for a fling. She's not even flirting. She only wants to be your friend, but you cut her off at every turn. Why?'' The trouble was, he'd met a lot of women who—well— who'd found him an enjoyable temporary diversion over the years. Until recently, that had been fine—beautiful women throwing themselves at him was every young man's fantasy.

But these women invariably dropped him to run off and marry some solid citizen. Zack was weary of being Mr. Last Fling. At this stage of his life, he wanted something more substantial. It had been good to reconnect with his brothers and get to know their families. He hadn't made progress with his dad, yet, but there was time.

Time.

He closed his eyes. Right now, he had nothing but time, and he was bored. Dinner was still an hour away. Marc was hard at work in the medical clinic and Mimi was in Portland chairing some ''Save the Planet'' meeting. Susan and Jake were overseeing work at the mine, their babies strapped to their backs. And George was taking his afternoon siesta.

Zack didn't know where Olivia had gone. He hadn't seen her since she'd stomped off in search of food, around one o'clock. He couldn't blame her for avoiding him. He'd been an ass. He'd experienced a painful surge of lust when she'd tumbled into his arms, so he'd fought it with ridicule. That had been unfair. How was it her fault too many pretty yuppies had sown their wild oats with him, only to move on to minivans and backyard barbecues?

How was it her fault that he'd led a wild, disobedient life, with the longest, wildest streak of disobedience being about sex. He'd done exactly as he pleased, and what pleased him was freewheeling, uncomplicated womanizing. After a while, though, all that lechery had left him haunted by the psychological harm it had done. He was finished with that life, and experiencing that familiar sexual stirring for Olivia had made him angry with himself. Damn his hide for taking it out on her.

Now, with a little time to reflect, he knew Olivia hadn't come here with a fling in mind. He cursed himself for spending even one split second *regretting* that she didn't want a fling. He hated himself for hesitating one moment to accept her platonic friendship. He shook his head in self-disgust. Narrowly eyeing the distant surf, he watched it roll over the beach, then retreat into the sea. He'd been staring for an hour, having heard such a tranquil view was supposed to be relaxing, but he wasn't relaxed.

Gritting out a raw oath, he hunched forward in the wicker chair, planting his forearms on his thighs. "What's the matter with you, Merit?" he muttered. "Why are you convicting her of crimes she hasn't committed? Or is your pride hurt because she *doesn't* want a quickie affair? And what if she did and you let it happen? How much worse would you feel when she walked away?'' He exhaled wearily. ''Are you nuts?''

''Who are you talking to?''

Olivia's question, coming from nearby, shook Zack, but he managed not to exhibit outward signs of shock— like leaping from his chair. After a count of three, he turned to give her a nod, hoping he didn't appear as idiotic as he felt. ''I'm talking to myself.'' He sat back. ''I have to admit, I'm fascinating.''

Knowing she deserved an apology, he motioned her forward. ''Look, I'm sorry about earlier. There's no excuse for my behavior. I guess I just took my boredom out on you.'' There could be an inkling of truth to that. He didn't know how much more of this peaceful island living he could endure.

She sat down in a wicker armchair across an iron coffee table surfaced with green tiles. ''Thanks. Let's forget it.'' She paused to cross her legs and Zack made a mental note of how very long and trim they were. Her cheeks pinkened and he had a physical reaction that was way out of proportion. Blast. She didn't have to flirt. She just had to show up.

''Say, Zack,'' she said, her glance suddenly furtive. For a brief, vivid instant her tongue flicked around her lips, wetting them. He shifted his attention to the rose garden, but the blossoms only reinforced his mental image of her pink cheeks and rosy lips.

''Uh—about what you said…''

He experienced a stab of guilt. ''I thought I apologized for that.''

''No—I mean, you did. But I've been thinking about what you said, and I was wondering…''

When she didn't say more, he met her eyes, puzzled.

What was she having such a hard time getting out. "What were you wondering?" he asked.

"Uh—er—I mean, you got me to thinking," she went on, then stopped and curled her hands in her lap, knotting her fingers together. "I've been thinking," she repeated.

Zack nodded. "I see." He didn't.

She giggled, the display clearly brought on by nerves, because there was no humor in it. "Actually—actually, I do have a point."

She cleared her throat and pulled her hands apart, then clasped the arms of her chair. He noted with some surprise that her knuckles had gone white. "It's like this," she said, taking a deep breath, "I'd like your help with something."

He frowned. What kind of help could she need from him? "You want me to lift something heavy?"

She stared for a heartbeat, then smiled. Apparently she thought he was kidding. "No—it's…" She opened her mouth, then closed it. He watched as a frown formed on her brow. "Look, Zack, it's not like I didn't already know this, someplace deep inside, but you made me face it. There's something I have to do." She stopped to look at him as though she wasn't sure how to go on.

He leaned forward, resting his forearms on his thighs. "You want me to kill somebody for you."

She laughed, the sound less one of exuberance than surprise. Nevertheless, it had a warming effect. "Zack, I'm trying to be serious. Don't tease." She presented him with a worried grimace. "Okay, I'll get to the point."

He clasped his hands loosely together and nodded, deciding to keep his trap shut.

"Zack…" She lifted her chin as though determined to get on with it. "You've made it very clear that I'm way too reserved and repressed. You were absolutely right when you said any woman who can't even walk on grass in high heels is so physically and emotionally throttled she should be tossed out into the real world for a good, harsh reality check.''

He heard what she said, but couldn't take her seriously. "I've never said a sentence that long in my life," he kidded.

She blinked, looking as though he'd slapped her. "Don't joke. I've thought about this a long, long time and I think you were right to mock me."

He glanced at his watch, then eyed her dubiously. "You consider four hours a long, long time?" He sat back. "Okay, what's the punch line?"

She vaulted up. "I mean it, Zack. You've made me see things about myself that I've avoided facing. I've been the repressed, dutiful daughter long enough. Deep down, I'm miserable. Maybe that's why I decided to try skydiving. I knew on some unconscious level what you've stated aloud. I need to loosen up. *A lot.* And—and, since you're the one pure hedonist I've ever met, and the man who made the truth so painfully clear, you owe it to me to help me learn to spread my wings."

Zack stared. He didn't know whether she'd meant to compliment him or insult him with that hedonist remark, but that didn't matter. What mattered was, she seemed serious. At least she *thought* she was. He decided she was going through some kind of recuperatory phase—her new strength causing her to overcompensate or overestimate. Something medical and probably common enough.

He decided to try to laugh it off. "Liv, sweetheart, apparently whatever medication Marc's been feeding you has some unsettling side effects. I think you should go back to bed." He shook his head at her.

"Are you now saying you don't think I need to get in touch with my wild side?"

He frowned. He had intimated that. And in all honesty, she was way too controlled. But that was for *his* taste. What did he know about financial wizards and presidential campaigns and how "wild" they could be and still function in their high-pressure, high-profile jobs? "I think you should leave well enough alone," he grumbled.

"I see," she snapped. "You're completely willing to make fun of me, but you refuse to help, is that it?" She swept him with a damning look. "Sure! Why not? It's easy to condemn, but it takes *backbone* to help." She pushed up from her chair, glaring. "I gave you more credit, Mr. Merit! And to think, I defended you to my father. I told him you weren't just a lazy playboy out for whatever you could get for the least effort!"

Stalking around the low table she jabbed at his chest with a fingernail. "You have some colossal nerve giving me your uninvited and hurtful opinions, then rejecting me when I ask you to help change what you, yourself, pointed out needed changing!"

He pushed up from the chair. "You're hysterical, Miss Nordstrom. When you feel better you'll realize this whole topic of conversation was absurd." He turned to go. *Ribbing her was megastupid, Merit! Look what you've done!*

"Wild" wasn't his thing these days. And helping Olivia Nordstrom develop her wild side was about as far from anything he planned to do as learning to needlepoint. He had problems of his own to deal with. The tranquil, quiet life on Merit island was driving him to distraction, yet he craved solidity and permanence. *Yep, Merit, you're nuts. You can't help this woman. You can't even figure yourself out.*

A tug on his arm cut through his musings. "Don't

dismiss me as if I were a child!'' She swung around to face him. ''I swear to you, Zack, I'm determined to do this. Since we're both stuck here on this island, why can't we work together? Please, show me how to get rid of the everlastingly Miss Refined-Studious-Obedient, and become a person with relish for living and a dramatic temperament.''

Zack frowned at her. She was certainly a striking picture, all wild-eyed and blushing. To look at her now, she already had passion and a dramatic temperament. A stirring sight. Even her pert nostrils flared. Fighting a wayward surge of attraction, he scowled at her. ''What would you do with this newfound wildness?'' he challenged. ''How would it help you as your father's financial guru?''

''That wouldn't change,'' she insisted. ''I can be wild and do my job.''

He grunted out a caustic chuckle. ''There's that wacky work ethic sneaking back in.'' He had an urge to caress her crimson cheek but squelched it. ''Face it, Liv, you're doomed to be a hardworking, stable woman and there's nothing you can do about it. I'm sorry I teased you. Forget everything I said. What the hell do I know?''

Her lips thinned, but even thinned they were bothersomely sensual. ''I thought you would understand if anybody did,'' she cried. ''Didn't you run away from home to find the real you? Haven't you lived the life you chose without apologizing to anybody?''

He didn't enjoy having his dubious choices thrown in his face as an argument in favor of recklessness. ''Yeah,'' he said, with a twisted grin. ''That's me. The plaster saint for selfish self-indulgence.'' He gave a mocking salute. ''I am *the* expert. But as the expert, I have to warn you, getting intimate with your wild side isn't all it's cracked up to be.''

She crossed her arms, looking adamant. "Well, neither is domestication. Ask any *cow*!"

He watched her with clamped teeth. This wasn't funny anymore. "You don't know what you're asking. You don't really want to be wild."

"But I do!" she retorted. "What do you think the skydiving was, if not a bid to break free?"

He shrugged, deciding not to bring up the fact that she almost died. "Ever do it again?"

"I did it twice before—before…"

"Yeah, but did you ever do it—after?"

She cast her gaze down. "I went white-water rafting, though." She glared at him. "And—and I went to a ka-rate class once."

"Once?" He lifted a cynical eyebrow.

Her exhale was a frustrated moan. "Daddy found out." She fisted her hands. "Zack, I need your *help*!"

One thing was sure. Her father had been a strong, sti-fling influence on her. Zack experienced a stab of com-passion, but fought it. She didn't really want to open that Pandora's box. With a slow, resolved shake of his head, he said, "You're not getting any wildness lessons from me."

They stared each other down for several ponderous seconds before she blurted, "Please! Help me see what life's like drenched with pleasure and passion! You could be my last chance!"

Her plea struck like the blunt end of a pickax. How wrong and simple could he be? The senator's daughter had a use for him, all right. She was just another preppy princess hankering to do the nasty with a wild man for a few hot nights before running back to daddy. Why had he thought she was different? *"Holy—"* He cut himself off. *Why me? Am I wearing a sign? Stud For Rent.* "Give me a freakin' break," he growled, pivoting away.

"No! I swear I'm going to do this!" She bolted to face him and grabbed his hands. "Kiss me, Zack!"

It wasn't as though the idea had never crossed his mind, but he was too furious, too disillusioned, maybe both. Or was he afraid if he allowed himself to weaken, he'd do exactly as she asked—*to blazes with the very real possibility she would regret her rashness next week!*

With a shrug he hoped looked more casual than it was, he said, "Give it up. You're not wild, and even if you were, I've outgrown wild women." Breaking eye contact, he made himself turn away.

"But you've known them! You know how they behave!" She grasped his wrist. "Would a wild woman let you get away with that?"

Before he could respond, she threw her arms around his neck and kissed him with a white-hot passion that only serious outrage could generate.

CHAPTER FOUR

ZACK had no plans to prolong Liv's impulsive act, and no intention of returning her kiss. Instinctively he lifted his hands to draw her arms from around his neck and end the craziness. Yet somehow, in the heartbeat between aim and accomplishment, sparks of unwanted excitement short-circuited his good intentions.

Pressed wantonly against him, Olivia's sensual onslaught sent fire raging along every nerve in his body. She clung to him. Her kiss, sweet and throbbing, hot and arousing, triggered a primal male urge for mastery—and release.

He wasn't clear on the time line of events, but he grew vaguely aware that his mouth had begun to move over hers, his kiss neither easy nor clever, but stormy and unwise.

Her lips opened, inviting intimate possession, and her nails bit into his back. A deep, aching pleasure filled him, so staggering no other experience in his life—no matter how wild or dangerous—could compare.

An explosion of sensations sang through him as their tongues danced and darted, delighted and dared. His need to fully unleash his hunger, to seek satisfaction, crescendoed. Her body was warm and welcoming; her fingers stroked, scraped, teased—*implored*—wreaking havoc on his willpower. His gut torqued, tightening until the sweet torture was unbearable.

He trailed his hands down her back, relishing every curve. When his tactile inquiry reached the roundness of her hips, he pressed her hard into him, his lust a palpable entity, heralding looming victory. He would be her man-trophy—willingly overcome. Zachary Merit, yet again, an enthusiastic sexual memento for some woman's memory book. Another piece of him, pleasantly plundered in the name of thrill-seeking.

He was no naïve innocent in the equation. He knew what he was doing, and he always did it with gusto. When in *blazes* would he find the grit to back off—to act on his conviction that this was wrong? Nobody benefited from such rash indulgence, though the harm could last a lifetime. How many times did he have to get burned to learn to keep the hell away from fire?

He doubted that Olivia could fully understand the downside of tasting reckless pleasure, coming from such a cloistered existence. Could he muster the stones to spare her that knowledge?

Marshaling what was left of his will, he slid his hands to her waist and pressed her away. Determined to put enough emotional distance between them so she would think twice before jumping into anything this stupid again, he dragged his mouth from hers, warning raggedly, "Don't ask for things you know nothing about, little girl." He gave her a grim look, trying to recover from the breathless tailspin of her kiss. "There are worse fates than being the neurotic daughter of a man who could be our next president."

He struggled to swim through the haze of feelings. Forcing his anger to the surface, he tamped down the heat of desire. Unfortunately its pain lingered, powerful and crippling. "Don't go jumping off any moral cliffs, Liv." Dragging an unsteady hand across his mouth in the vain attempt to banish her taste, he swerved away. To put distance between them, he tramped onto the lawn where her scent couldn't screw with his head and the shimmer in her eyes didn't turn his belly sour with longing.

Olivia was so stunned by the power of Zachary's kiss, she couldn't think straight. She'd been kissed before, but...

She staggered a step sideways, then backward. The only reason she didn't collapse to the stone floor was that she stumbled against a wicker chair and fell to the cushioned seat. Hardly registering that she was sitting down, or caring how she got there, she tried to make sense of what happened.

The one thing she was sure about—besides her devastating reaction to his kiss—was his equally devastating rejection. Her brain began to come out of its strange shock, and humiliation took hold. She cringed and hunched forward. Burying her face in her hands, she choked back a sob. Hadn't she *already* learned the lesson about how being daring can injure—even kill—when her parachute hadn't opened?

She sucked in a shuddery breath. Then why was she so stunned to discover that throwing herself at Zack— though his reputation implied that he indulged in such distractions daily—might be as hazardous as jumping out of an airplane?

It wasn't only his rejection that shocked her, but the fact that such a live-for-thrills animal as Zachary Merit should lecture her on morality! That stung like a slap! *How dare he!*

She sucked in another breath, indignation billowing with the fresh supply of oxygen. "How dare you!" she blurted, shooting a deadly look around.

Where was he?

She pushed up from the chair, fisted her hands on her

hips and peered around the lawn and expansive gardens. She spied him, fifty feet away, heading toward the beach. *"How dare you!"* she shouted.

He faltered for a half-step, then continued on. She chewed her lower lip. "If you think I'll just disappear, you're crazy, Mr. Merit!" Heading at a near-run out of the loggia's shelter, she shouted, "How dare you lecture me on morals! You! One of the top ten American bachelors contending for Sybarite of the Year!"

He halted, shifting to glower over one shoulder. "You can't insult me with your high-dollar vocabulary, sweetheart," he said. "I didn't graduate magna cum smart-ass, so you might as well use plain English."

"Okay, how plain is this?" She caught up with him. "You have your nerve giving me advice on morality! And—and what did you mean by *neurotic*!"

His half smile mocked her. "If you understand the word *sybarite*, you understand neurotic." He shook his head as though finding her to be beyond hope. "Go away, little girl."

"Quit calling me *little girl*!" Thrusting out her chin, she dared, "Are you all show and no go, Mr. Merit?"

His expression changed from antagonistic to dubious. "What are you babbling about?"

She smirked, a weird kind of courage washing over her. What more could he do to her? How much worse could his rejection get? She'd been served up the worst of it, why not fight and scrape with her last ounce of pride? She didn't want to go on being the regimented automaton she'd been for twenty-four years. She wanted to be a living, breathing woman, who could take life by the ears and wrestle it to its knees. "I'm saying, I'm starting to doubt the hype about you. All these years, how have you gotten away with making people think you're a wild man? Do you have a Houdini of a press agent who's made the phony behind the curtain look like a wizard?''

His eyebrows drew farther down. He started to speak, and Liv held her breath, hoping her goading had done its work. But he seemed to think better of whatever he'd been about to say and turned away, dismissing her with an impatient wave.

This time his rejection made her crazily furious—and feisty. She didn't know why, but Zachary brought out the passion—*no*—temper in her like nobody in the world. Rushing to his side, she grabbed his arm. ''What do I have to do to get your help? Why do you dislike me so much you can't even do me *one* little favor?''

He stopped. ''One *little* favor?'' He glared at her. ''You think using me as some kind of kinky sex surrogate for the few days you're here is a little favor?''

His challenge stunned her—not only because he made it clear what a huge sacrifice it would be to make love to her, but because the idea had never occurred to her— well, not on a conscious level. Though, she had to admit, the brazen kiss she'd planted on him had come from somewhere.

Her burning cheeks told her she was blushing as furiously as was humanly possible without bursting into flame. ''I don't want a…kinky sex surrogate!'' she choked out. ''Sex with you is the absolute *last* thing on my mind!'' That statement wasn't the truest thing she'd ever said, but for her present intent, it was factual enough. ''Besides, just out of curiosity, since when did you become a monk?''

''The last thing on your mind, huh?'' His jaw muscles clenched. ''Maybe it's none of my business, Miss

Nordstrom, but…'' He indicated the loggia with a broad wave. "What was that lip-lock all about?''

She was unhappy he brought that up. Dismay swept over her when she realized she had no explanation. With a brief, wary hesitation, she shrugged and improvised, "Well—well, I was frantic to get your attention.''

His skeptical expression and lack of response ate at her depleted reserves. She cast her gaze toward the surf, then made herself face him again. "What would you rather I did?" she asked, "Kick you, or hit you with a chair?''

Desperate, she threw out her arms. "I need you, Zack." Her voice broke, and she blinked, fighting tears. She didn't want to break down. His opinion of her was too close to rock bottom already. "I—I need you to help me. I swear I won't embarrass you again by throwing myself at you. I just need…" She couldn't finish her sentence and keep her appeal free of quavering sadness, so she closed her mouth. A tear escaped, but she swiftly wiped it away.

Struggling to get a grip on her emotions, she realized if she planned to keep from turning into a blubbering heap, she'd better fall back on her upbringing—attempt calm logic. Obviously flinging herself bodily at him hadn't been the right course, and considering his reaction, certainly not one in which she had any expertise.

She cleared her throat and met his gaze, disapproving, but different somehow. "Just show me how to free up, to be a little more spontaneous—in everyday things," she said quietly. Taking a step away from him, she smiled, hoping the act looked more real than it felt. "No touching. I promise.''

He watched her, his frown contemplative. His silent inspection went on and on, so long that it was enough to give the screaming meemies to a person who wasn't *already* tottering on the edge of hysteria. After what seemed like a lifetime, he sucked in a breath and crossed his arms over his chest. *"Damn!"* His tone was ripe with misgiving. "This is dumb." He flicked his gaze to the sky. "If I weren't so everlastingly bored, I wouldn't even consider it."

When he faced her again, his slow nod was accompanied by an acrimonious flare of nostrils. It was the most grudging yes she'd ever witnessed. Even so, her heart did a high kick of gratitude.

"Okay," he muttered. "But don't think you'll have any picnic. I'll bait you to the limits of your endurance, if for no other reason than to prove there isn't a wild bone in your body." His features hard, eyes glinting with defiance, he held out a hand. "Agreed?" The query was definitely a dare.

She stared, flummoxed by his threat to prove her incorrigibly prim. A burst of indignation aided in her quick recovery. To demonstrate an utter lack of desire to touch him, she planted her hands on her hips and exhibited a saucy smirk. "Agreed." She nodded curtly. "How do we start?"

He swept her with a calculating look. "First…" His lips twisted in a grin that made the back of her neck prickle with foreboding. "We lose the clothes."

Olivia stared at herself in the full-length mirror of her room. She didn't look like she belonged among lovely antiques. "I'd blend in better on some street corner soliciting johns." She grimaced at her reflection, grudgingly admitting it wasn't really that bad. She simply wasn't accustomed to wearing the current clingy, belly-baring, cropped-tops-skirts-and-pants that were so popular.

Susan and Mimi had embraced the "exploring Liv's wild side" experiment with relish and had volunteered an assortment of up-to-the-minute outfits that would rival anything the current hot Hollywood stars were modeling on covers of the slickest women's magazines.

Even so, Olivia felt half dressed. She stared at herself, scandalized. She was an accountant and the daughter of a conservative senator. She'd dressed for those roles for what seemed like forever. For all her adult life, her knees were only allowed a peek at daylight when she sat down. Even then she managed to manipulate her hem to cover them.

In this clingy skirt, she could see every bend and bulge, and every breath she breathed. When she sat down—if she got up the nerve—this tiny garment had no hope of coming anywhere near her knees.

The sweater blouse sported a respectable jewel neckline and short sleeves. It was just too tight and four inches too short. Though she wasn't particularly big busted, the sweater made sure the world would know she was definitely a woman. Her stomach showed, pasty white from years without benefit of sunshine.

She tugged on the pink fabric, but the wayward knit bounced back, insisting on displaying her belly button as though it were some national treasure on display. She hiked up her skirt's waistband, but it, too, had a mind of its own and slithered down to hover at an indecent level on her hips.

She eyed herself with misgivings. She didn't show this much leg when she wore shorts! Yanking on the hem of her skirt, she struggled to make it longer, but it too rejected her attempt. No way would it become the knee-length linen suit skirt she willed it to be.

A knock on her door brought her head up with a start, making her totter in her open-toed platforms. With a grab at the dresser, she regained her balance. "Who is it?" Apprehension edged her voice. She didn't dare let anybody to see her this way! Why, oh why, did Mimi and Susan neglect to supply her with a nice, double-breasted, ankle-length jacket?

"Zack."

It would be him! She made a face. "What do you want?"

"I'm selling Girl Scout cookies—what do you think I want?"

Her stomach turned over. After a quick reassessment of herself in the mirror she shook her head. "Do you want to see what I look like?"

"Amazing guess."

"Why?" Nervously she toyed with a strand of her hair.

"Because you asked for my help and I'm here to help. Why do you think?"

She grimaced. "Oh…right."

"It's time for dinner," Zack called through the door.

She squeezed her eyes tight. Not only did she have to let him see her dressed like this, but she had to eat dinner—in front of everybody—belly button and all!

"Liv?" Zack coaxed, when she didn't respond. "Why do I have a feeling you've already changed your mind about this favor you begged me to help you with?"

He was too close to being right for her peace of mind. She felt idiotic and hated herself for her hesitation. He was already taunting her, baiting her, as he'd said he would. She'd made a fool of herself by asking for his help. Was she going to get *nothing* out of all that groveling and pleading? Was she really the hopeless, neurotic, prim little girl he said she was? Couldn't she even wear fashionable clothes without freaking?

She straightened her shoulders. *Not in this lifetime, mister!* "I'm coming!" she shouted, sneaking a last, morbidly curious peek in the mirror.

She swung open the door, glaring, expecting to see him burst out laughing. But that wasn't his reaction. He merely gave her a long look. A long, serious, thoughtful look. After a moment his eyebrows knit slightly.

"Don't frown at me like that," she groused. "I'm completely—fine."

"I didn't say you weren't," he muttered.

She looked down at herself, then back at him. "But— you made a face."

"Yeah, well, what do you want, applause?" He startled her when he tugged on her earlobe. "What's with the little pearl earrings? Who do you think you are, Miss Debutante of 1972?"

Before she could stop him, he'd slipped off one earring. "Don't you have anything flashier?"

She grabbed the jewelry out of his hand. "I have a shoehorn in my purse." Annoyed, she jabbed the pearl back on her ear.

He passed her a quick, aggravated look. "We'll let that go for now." He indicated her wrist. "The watch has to go."

She instinctively placed a protective hand over the leather band. "Why?"

He walked further into the room. "Free spirits don't care what time it is, sweetheart."

She frowned. When he started to unfasten her watch, she jerking her arm away. She didn't like the thrill rushing along her spine with his touch, especially since he was removing personal items from her body as though he had some proprietary claim. Was she ill? Was the iron she was taking for her anemia driving her insane? She'd have to ask Marc about side effects.

"We said no touching," she reminded. "You're making pretty free with the hands."

He stepped back. "Okay, you take it off. I'll deal with the hair."

"What hair?" She had a bad feeling. "Not *my* hair?"

"Take off the watch and shut up." He rummaged in the dresser drawers and she glowered at his back. Somewhere in midglower, it occurred to her that he looked scrumptious in chinos, especially from behind. He had exceptional, tight buns. She cringed at the wayward thought. She hardly ever noticed men's buns. *Why his?* And the cotton shirt, though not tight, hugged his shoulders. That expanse of anatomy that supported his head seemed awfully broad, for shoulders. She touched a finger to her lips in contemplation. It was probably just the way he was standing that made them seem disproportionately wide.

He shifted to the other side of the dresser, and she squinted at him. No. Those shoulders were easily wider than most. Exhaling a disgruntled sigh, she tilted her head, focusing on one of his arms. The flex and pull of muscle as he opened drawers, riffled around, then closed—

"Here we go." He turned around and held up a large pewter-colored hair clip. "Now twist all that stuff in a knot and fasten it with this."

She eyed the clip with distaste. "What's the matter with wearing my hair down?" It was a simple, tidy shoulder-length and she liked it the way it was.

He pursed his lips, clearly skeptical. "Are we balking, Miss Nordstrom?" He wagged the clip before her eyes, his manner purposefully taunting. "Lots of people wouldn't even consider this a yawn, let alone wild."

"This is ridiculous," she mumbled, reaching up to twist her hair into an unruly lump. "Give me the darn thing!" She snatched it from his fingers and clamped it over the mass. It felt weird and drooped to her nape, but she decided the way she wore her hair wasn't worth arguing over. "Satisfied?"

"Now that's wild hair." He winked, and she felt strangely buoyant. *Buoyant?* She balled her fists, crushing the feeling.

"About the watch…"

Irritated with both herself and with him, she determinedly fumbled with her watch band. After several drawn-out seconds, she managed to unfasten it. Eyeing him with a mixture of mistrust and tenacity, she tossed it on the dresser. "You're not proving me a hopeless fuddy-duddy, no matter how hard you try! Now let's go down to dinner!"

Zack escorted Olivia downstairs. "If anybody laughs at me, I'll kill you," she grumbled.

He glanced her way. She knew it, rather she sensed it, since she refused to look at him. "A wild woman wouldn't care, sweetheart."

Tugging at her dress hem, she shot him a grumpy frown. Would she ever learn to keep her mouth shut? Was she determined to set herself up over and over for his heckling? Where had her wide streak of self-abuse come from?

She could feel her hair unwinding and reached up to catch it. "Oh—drat."

"Hold still," he said. "I'll fix it."

She peered at him. "I don't think so."

"Think again." He plucked the clip from her hand then angled her so her back was to him. His fingers brushed her nape as he swept her hair up. The light touch tingled, registering all the way to her toes. Not until he'd clipped the stuff into a secure ball did she realize she'd stopped breathing. "There," he said. "That should hold."

He indicated that they move on. At long last she managed to inhale, hating her erotic reaction. "Did you learn that in hairdresser school?" she taunted, trying to make him as uncomfortable as he was making her.

"I pack parachutes, sweetheart. Fastening hair is a piece of cake."

He flicked her a narrow glance and she wondered at his mood. He should be having a high old time, but he seemed afflicted. He frowned at her for another split second before he indicated the dining room. "I hope you like your dinner. A wild woman would."

She had a bad feeling. It got worse when they entered the cavernous dining room and nobody else was there. Liv nervously scanned the long table. Places were set for seven, so why were they alone? "Where is everybody else?"

Zack apparently anticipated her reluctance, because he took her arm. Though his grip wasn't painful, she couldn't wriggle out of it. "Come on." He tugged her toward the table. "The first course is just for you."

"What is it? I don't do drugs."

He halted before a chair and released her. She waited for him to assist her to sit. When he took the seat next to her, she looked down at him, puzzled. He'd been polite enough to help seat her when he'd eaten at her parents' home. He didn't smile as he indicated the chair. "Climb in, Wild Woman."

With an irked throat-clearing, she shoved the heavy antique chair back and seated herself, then struggled to slide forward, bouncing and pulling, bouncing and pulling. She shifted to look at Zack, and noticed he'd lifted a covered dish of ornate sterling, ignoring her plight.

"Does discovering my wilder side mean you have to be a jerk?" She happened to glance down to discover her skirt had ridden up dangerously. Wriggling around she managed to tug it down, at least a little. Hurriedly she covered her too-bare legs with the linen napkin, blessing whoever decided on these great big ones.

"Jerk?" Zack placed the large dish beside her plate. "Think of it as a learning experience." He took the lid off the sterling dish and indicated the food. "Have some."

She eyed the lumpy, brownish-gray muck. "What is it?"

"A delicacy Mimi brought back from Tasmania." He lifted the serving spoon and portioned out a heaping blob, emptying it on her plate. "I can't remember the Tasmanian name, but here we call it Pig's trotters hash."

She was starving, so she'd picked up her fork. When his remark penetrated, she dropped it to her plate where it clanked deafeningly in the stillness. "Pig's *what*?" She stared at him.

He served himself a helping. "No, Pig's trotters—as in feet. Pig's trotters hash." He picked up his fork and dug in, glancing her way. "I like to call it a *taste* of wildness." He took a bite and winked, the act more contemptuous than playful.

She watched him, feeling ill. He took another forkful, then indicated her plate. "What are you waiting for?"

She could feel her face, frozen in horror—her nose wrinkled, her brow puckered in abhorrence, her mouth screwed up with revulsion. "Why isn't everybody else eating this?"

Zack took another bite. "Because Pig's trotters hash is an acquired taste."

"But if Mimi likes it so much, then—"

"She's pregnant." Zack gave her a you-should-know-better look. "You wouldn't ask a pregnant woman to eat feet."

She eyed heaven. "I wouldn't ask a garbage disposal to eat feet!"

"I see." Laying aside his fork, he sat back to eye her solemnly. "So far I've given you extremely simple tasks, Miss Nordstrom. Are you ready to forgo this search for your inner wild child?"

She opened her mouth, then closed it, clamped it. Crossing her arms she presented him with her most withering look. "You think you're so smart."

He lifted a shoulder and let it drop, the move alarmingly sexy, which only made her more furious.

"I'm quite a bit older than you are, Liv," he said. "I may not have gone to Yale, but I know people. You're not the pig-foot eating type. You're not the tight sweater and short skirt type, either. I can see how miserable you are. Why don't you admit it? Conservatism isn't a sin."

Stone-faced, she peered at him, incensed. Pulpy pig feet, of all things! She'd thought the clothes-thing was silly, but this was mean. Still, he'd eaten it. She glanced at her plate, almost convincing herself she could see bits of hoof. Swallowing bile, she shifted to glare at him.

His lips twisted in a cynical smile of victory.

That did it! He was *not* winning. He was not going to get away with calling her a neurotic little girl for the rest of her stay on Merit Island! For that matter, she couldn't stay if that were to be her fate. She pinched her lower lip between her teeth. Thinking about going back to the rat race made her feel faint. She wasn't up to that, yet.

A rock and a hard place. She certainly knew what that old saw meant now. She was wedged between them, and it was no party.

She stirred in her chair, cogitating on the blob on her plate. After a bleak few seconds, she passed Zack a guarded look. He'd eaten the horrid pig parts and he looked okay. *He looks delicious*, some imp in her mind corrected. Biting off an unattractive word, she turned away to get herself back on track.

"Did you say something to me?" he asked.

Her awkward vulnerability to him made her mad. With thinned lips she wagged her head.

"Are you sure?" he pressed. "I thought I heard—"

"You know exactly what I said," she bit out, scooping up her fork. "And if you don't want it permanently chiseled into your forehead with a fork, then drop it!"

Refusing to dwell on what she was about to do, she shut her eyes and shoveled a heap of the clotted glop into her mouth. She swallowed and cringed, expecting an aftertaste appropriate to fare that had spent its prefood days slopping around in barnyards. Whatever she'd expected, it didn't come. She opened her eyes, wondering at the pleasant texture and sticky-sweet flavor. It really wasn't bad.

She peered at Zack, who watched her silently. Long black lashes rode at half-mast across his eyes, a subtle seduction. *Excruciatingly subtle*, her brain jeered, *considering it hasn't been three hours since he made it clear he doesn't want anything physical going on between us!*

"Well?" he finally asked, leaning forward. "I hope you don't expect cheers. So you choked down one bite. Big deal."

She twisted away and clanked her fork on her plate. "I think I liked you better when you were bored."

A noise caught Olivia's attention and she glanced toward the entry as the rest of the clan entered.

"You're already eating?" Jake asked, as he moved to the opposite side of the table. He did a double take when he first glimpsed her, then grinned. "I like the sweater."

Heat crept up her cheeks.

"She's bringing out her wild side," Mimi chimed in.

Jake chuckled. "From what I can see, she's doing fine."

"Oh, you," Mimi giggled. "Typical male reaction to a tight sweater." She reached Olivia, touching her shoulder with affection. "You really do look wonderful. Jake's remark is proof. He's usually oblivious to women, except for Susan." Mimi smiled as Jake helped his wife with her chair.

"I agree with Jake," Susan said. "That color of pink is wonderful with your complexion, Liv."

"How do *you* like her complexion, Zack?" Mimi asked.

Olivia watched Zack's jaw clench, but he didn't speak.

Mimi laughed. "That much, huh?" She turned to Olivia. "I'll translate. Zack's crazy about your—um—complexion, too. Men are big on complexions." When her glance fell on Olivia's plate, her expression grew puzzled, then delighted. "Oh, I didn't know we were having rice pudding!" She clapped her hands and moved past Zack to her chair, where Marc helped her take her seat.

Flustered with embarrassment over the complexion remarks, Olivia stared after Mimi, confused, then looked at her plate. "What do you mean, rice pudding?" She indicated her food. "You're not talking about this, are you?"

Mimi nodded. "It's my favorite." She glanced at Zack. "How wild of you to eat dessert first." She wagged her fingers in the direction of the serving dish. "I think I will, too."

Olivia scowled at Zack. "Rice pudding?"

He leaned toward her and whispered, "Now I remember. That's what they call it in Tasmania." One eyebrow slowly arched, as if to say *gotcha*!

"What...a...contemptible...trick!" she charged under her breath. Fuming, she kicked him in the shin.

He closed one eye in a grimace that Olivia found quite entertaining. "What in Hades was that?" he growled.

"I don't know what they call it in Tasmania," she said, looking as composed as her smug merriment would allow, "but I like to think of it as *Your Just Desserts*!"

CHAPTER FIVE

ZACK certainly wasn't bored any longer. The mere fact that Liv had been showing off a great deal of skin these past couple of days had been enough to slice his boredom level in half.

Half?

Making a pained face, he amended that. Whether she wore an undersized sweater or a short-and-skimpy top, every blasted thing revealed each delectable curve and more or less of her midsection. *Mainly more.* He was beginning to think there was a conspiracy afoot to showcase her navel. If he were to be grimly honest, boredom had disappeared off the list of feelings that had pestered him for the past forty-eight endless hours.

He'd never been a man to embrace the perks of boredom, but right now he could give a passionate speech in homage to monotony. Boredom, Zack discovered, had its upside. To be bored meant *not* being in close proximity to a dainty, sexy nymphet, oblivious to his discomfort, parading around in "catch-me-sailor" costumes. She was making his self-imposed monkish existence hard to endure.

Blast the woman! She was even starting to enjoy the skimpy outfits highlighting her slim waist and damnably coy navel. Her initial embarrassment had lulled him into a false sense of security. He'd almost tasted victory that first night—almost. But he wasn't so sure any longer. Blast! If he hadn't been so convinced she would fade in the first round, he wouldn't have agreed to this foolishness. Making her wear faddishly skimpy styles was turning out to be a bad idea, more disturbing to his peace of mind than anything.

Had she considered her parents in all this? How would they embrace this inner "wild child" she was working so hard to unearth? He knew better than most about estrangement. He and his father had passed only a few cool words during his stay on the island, their breach seemingly too broad to span. He was sad, but not surprised.

What if Liv actually intended to become more free-spirited, no matter how tough the transition? What if this experiment led her to quit her job in her father's campaign? What if her physical and emotional mutation caused an estrangement between Liv and her parents, and she found herself suddenly without their love and support?

At least Zack had managed to rekindle a familial warmth with his brothers and their families. What would happen to Liv, an only child? *"No!"* he muttered, the vision too unsettling. Edgy and aggravated, he swung around to pace in the opposite direction over the den's oriental rug.

Olivia was going through some post-graduate, pre-White House rebellion, probably normal for people in her situation. "Soon enough, she'll get sick of this loosening up nonsense," he mumbled. "She'll throw on her high-heel pumps and her designer suit and hightail it back to Daddy."

"What are you mumbling about, boy?" George's voice boomed from behind Zack. "If you're speaking to me, speak up like a man."

Zack stiffened, his father's tirade pelting him like a hailstorm, hurtful and all too familiar. Imposing iron control, he shifted to face the older man. His expression as placid as he could manage, he nodded. "Hi, Dad."

George stood in the double-doored entry, his features florid. Zack recognized the old tyrant's fighting-cock stance—legs braced, fists on his hips, chin jutted. All this, plus his ruddy scowl, didn't leave much doubt that he was spoiling for a battle. He'd probably been building this head of steam for the past week.

Well, it wasn't going to happen. Zack had no plans to quarrel with his father. Not anymore. No matter what. "You're looking fit, Dad." He grinned, a monumental effort, and motioned his father forward. "We haven't had a chance to talk. Come on in."

George harrumped. "That's ironic, coming from you. We haven't had a chance to talk, *indeed*! You're the one who ran away for twenty years, breaking your mother's heart." He lifted a fist and shook it. "How could you have been so thoughtless and selfish?"

Guilt stabbed at Zack, and he grieved again for the loss of his mother, all those years forfeited with her by running away. Unable to hold onto his smile, he solemnly faced his father. "You'll never know how sorry I am."

George's caustic laugh grated, drawing fresh blood from the gaping wound in Zachary's heart. "*Sorry* is right. You're a very sorry specimen." George stalked toward his son. "You—the brightest, most promising of all my sons." He threw out his arms, his gestures broad and angry. "Brilliant but erratic, your teachers called you. Bored, restless and disruptive in class, but a *genius*, they said!" His angry shouts sprayed spittle like bullets. "So much potential for greatness, they insisted. And what do you do but throw it all away on wild, libidinous living. I'm ashamed, boy," he said. "Every time I look at what you are, what you've become, I am ashamed to call you my son.''

Sick desolation rushed through Zachary. *I am ashamed to call you my son.* The vicious declaration boomed, making his head ache. *I am ashamed to call you my son.*

Zack fought a growing fear that there might be nothing he could do or say to mend the split between him and his father. The breach formed over a twenty-year span seemed too wide, too deep. Had too many sorrows, disappointments come and gone between father and son to allow Zachary any hope for a relationship—or even that he might deserve a second chance?

"That's right. Stand there looking stubborn," George yelled. "I suppose you think racing boats, backpacking up mountains and chasing women is important work, worthy of your great gift. Good Lord, Zachary, you could have been a doctor like Marc or a captain of industry like Jake. With your brilliant mind you *could* have saved lives or done something innovative, groundbreaking—'' His voice cracked, his eyes shimmering with rage and pain.

Witnessing how deeply he'd hurt his father, Zack experienced a suffocating tightening of his throat. He couldn't speak, could hardly breathe.

"How long must you torture me by loafing around here?" his father asked, his voice low and gruff. "How long must I suffer your aimless presence, when every moment is a reminder of what might have…'' His voice died in a ragged croak. Shaking his head, he turned away.

"Dad," Zachary called. "Don't go." He found himself moving forward, grasping his father's arm and drawing him back. "You old reprobate," he murmured. "You're made of petrified wood and bad manners, but I love you. Maybe I don't deserve your forgiveness, but I can't—I won't leave here without trying to make amends.'' His father's grim countenance made him sick inside, but he wouldn't let his sorrow and regret deter him. Pulling his dad into his arms, he hugged him close. ''For whatever time we have left on this earth, Dad, and for whatever it's worth, I'm here for you. All I want—''

''You want! *You* want!'' His father shuddered and drew in a sharp breath. ''Here's what *I* want!'' He shoved from Zachary's grip. ''Just stay out of my way, boy!''

George spun away, but Zack caught him. ''Dad,'' he said, grasping his shoulder to stay his departure. The old man wouldn't look at him, and new anguish seared his gut. ''I hope, if you ever change your mind…'' he whispered roughly, ''that it won't be too late—for both of us.''

''Bah!'' George threw up an arm, dislodging Zachary's hold, and barreled out of the room. ''You're *dead* to me, boy,'' he shouted. ''Dead and gone!''

George's footsteps echoed along the hallway and finally disappeared. Shell-shocked by the bitterness of his father's rejection, Zachary stood unmoving for a long time. Biting regret twisted his belly and he tasted blood. He had no idea how much time passed before he gathered himself together enough to move. Shoving his hands through his hair, he exhaled heavily. ''Right—sure, whatever you say.''

''What are you muttering about?''

The sound of Jake's voice jarred Zachary and he stilled to peer at his brother. Jake lounged against the jamb of the den's entry, his grin bothersome. ''Let me take a wild guess,'' he went on. ''You're muttering something about the senator's daughter?''

Zack scowled. Only one other topic disturbed him as much as his father's hostility, and Jake had to zero in on it. "Don't you have work to do?" He glanced at his wristwatch. "It's just past two."

Jake lifted a casual shoulder. "Equipment trouble. We had to shut down for the day."

Zack broke eye contact. His brother's smirk was irritating the fire out of him. "Yeah, well, we all have our little problems, don't we?"

"Speaking of little problems, where *is* Miss Nordstrom?"

Zack sat down heavily on the sofa that faced the stone hearth. He glared into space. This was the last thing he needed right now. "How in blazes should I know where she is?" He expelled an exasperated breath.

"I haven't seen Susan since before noon," Jake said. "Or Mimi."

Zack stared into the fireplace where greenery had been artfully arranged. "I went rappelling this morning over on the south bluff, so I haven't seen anybody since breakfast."

"That's a bad sign—all of them missing, together." Jake chuckled, but Zack resisted the urge to turn. "I wonder what those three are cooking up?"

"Whatever it is, it had better not expose Liv's navel," Zack mumbled.

"What?"

"Nothing." Zack slumped against the cushion, lolling his head on the back of the couch.

The sound of footsteps told him his brother was approaching rather than leaving, as he'd silently commanded. "It sounded like you said something about Liv's navel."

Zack cringed, wishing his brother didn't have the hearing of a Great Dane. "While I was rappelling I fell on my head. I'm probably babbling gibberish."

"That's one theory," Jake said, taking a seat on the far end of the couch. Though Zack refused to look, he felt his brother's speculative stare. "That little navel getting to you?"

Zack flicked a narrowed gaze toward Jake. *"What?"*

Jake's expression was amused. "I know you've been trying to keep your hands off her." He shifted to better face his brother, slinging an arm along the back of the couch. "She's a pretty intimidating woman. Yale honors graduate. Beautiful. Her father is one of the most powerful men in the country." He nodded, all humor vanishing from his expression. "Any guy would feel daunted around her." He leaned nearer and clapped Zack on the shoulder. "If you want my guess, man, I think she likes you. But I understand your hesitation to get involved. Being in love with a woman like Liv Nordstrom would be like trying to hold a tiger by the tail."

The shock of Jake's remark hit full force and Zack jumped up. "In love!" He glared, incredulous. "I'm not in love with her! I have no intention of being in love with her." He stalked to the fireplace and clenched his fingers around the cold stone mantel. "Are you nuts?" He glared over his shoulder, then turned to face his brother with a don't-even-go-there scowl.

Appearing unscathed by Zack's killing stare, Jake lounged back. "It's not a sin to be in love with an exceptional woman, Bro." A corner of his mouth quirked. "The sin is, that you don't believe you're good enough for her."

Zack's scowl froze. His throat went dry and he was momentarily speechless. Working to regain his composure, he ground out, "You *are* nuts!"

Jake pushed up from the couch and ambled over to give his brother a friendly thump on the arm. "If you care for her, let her know. If you don't tell her, you could regret it for the rest of your life.''

''Care for her?'' Zack couldn't believe what he was hearing and grew irritated by his brother's idiotic assumption. ''The sooner she's out of my hair, the better I'll like it!'' Angry, and not sure why, he pushed past Jake, only to spin to confront him. He opened his mouth to argue his point, but nothing came. Why couldn't he think straight?

His head swarmed with brief flashes of Liv—her face, her lips, the warm, honey-brown of her eyes, her smile and, yes, her maddening navel. The images danced before his mind's eye, hazy or clear, some even too brief to comprehend, taunted and harassed him. No woman had ever affected him so bizarrely. He mouthed a curse, spun away and stalked out of the room.

Then he ran smack into a woman. Since he could see Susan and Mimi directly behind the bundle he'd slammed up against, he had a sinking feeling the softly curvy being in his arms might be... ''Liv?'' he asked, his voice croaky from the collision.

Of course it was Liv! He'd only had two kinds of luck lately, bad and none at all. He'd instinctively wrapped his arms around her when they collided, and now his hands were spreading *very stupidly* across a warm, silky back.

''Ouch!'' she cried. ''You're on my foot!''

Before he registered what she said, he lurched away in an attempt to remove temptation. *''Damn!''* He glanced at her feet. She wore black ankle boots. ''Sorry.'' He wasn't in the mood to deal with her right now. He needed to be alone, to work on his composure. Between Olivia's unwitting seductiveness and George's undisguised loathing, Zack felt like he'd been mauled by a pride of lions.

The idea of looking into her eyes troubled him. "I need to go…" he mumbled, turning away. "Do—this thing…"

"Wait," Susan called, catching him by the arm. "Don't you have anything to say about Liv's hair?"

He shifted to eye Susan, worrying that he wasn't all that sharp at the moment. Running bodily into Liv seemed to have dulled his brain—at least it dulled the brain he was supposed to do his thinking with. "Her—hair?"

Susan grinned. "Her hair." She gestured with a hand. "It's wild."

Zack reluctantly faced Olivia. Today she wore what looked like a black slip that hit her too far above the knees. A skinny red sweater stretched across her shoulders and hooked beneath her breasts by an extremely fortunate button. For once, her navel was hidden from his view. Talk about a break. He inhaled, experiencing a surge of relief as he raised his examination to her hair—beautiful black stuff he'd itched to feel dangling down, tickling his chest as she rode him hard—

What he saw stunned him as thoroughly as if he'd been belted in the gut with a brick. "What did you do to it?"

Olivia looked at him with an inquisitive expression as she reached up and fluffed her hair. Short and shaggy, it sported a white streak that ran from jagged bangs back as far as he could see. Without daring to comment further, he walked around her to check out the back. As he feared, it was cut so short he could see her nape, where one longer, chalk-colored sprig dangled.

"My Lord," he ground out. "You look like Pepe Le Pew."

"Gee, thanks." She faced him. "I was going for the cartoon skunk look."

Scandalized, and amazed he could actually *be* scandalized, he stared at Liv for another heartbeat, then shifted his glare to her coconspirators. "I can't believe you two thought this was a good idea."

Mimi laughed. "Don't you love it?"

With an unbelieving shake of his head, he indicated Liv's mutilated hair. "She has to go back to California next week. She has to be in front of the press. Her father could be our next president!" He looked at Liv hoping he'd been hallucinating. No, it was still bad. He eyed heaven. "Have you all lost your minds?"

"For a hedonist, Zack, you're a real prude," Liv said, drawing his scowl. She plunked her fists on her hips and he noticed her nails were now the color of smog. Doubtless a nervier hue than she'd ever sported, and unquestionably uglier. "You should be applauding my bravery!" she insisted.

"I *should* be spanking your backside, young lady. It's one thing to wear unconservative clothes, but to destroy your hair?" He clamped his jaws, tamping down his wrath. She'd had such beautiful hair! "What were you thinking?"

Susan burst out laughing, and Zack shot his attention to her. A second later, Mimi joined in. Perplexed Zack peered at the blonde, then shifted his frown to Olivia in time to see her lips twitch. She grabbed her hair and jerked it off to reveal dark, unmutilated locks, pulled back in a knot. "Kidding!" she shouted, joining in the tittering.

Provoked, Zack glared at Olivia for a long moment. Why had the idea that she'd cut her hair made him so angry? "Cute," he muttered, feeling like a fool. "You're three funny females." He'd had enough! Pinning Olivia with a stern look, he muttered, "I knew this was nothing

to you but a game. You're exactly what I said—*a fake
free-spirit.*"

"Is that worse than being a fake thrill-seeker?" she
charged, her amusement as dead as if it had never existed.

Deep laughter coming from behind Zack made it clear
Jake had joined them in the hall. "She asks a good question," he said.

Zack ignored his brother's jibe. He knew what Jake
meant—that if he didn't care about Liv, he'd be all over
her—Yale grad or not, hair or no hair. Blast it! Little did
Jake know that…that…what? *Damn, why couldn't he
think straight lately?*

He eyed Liv, experiencing a new flood of determination to get her off the island and out of his life. This was
not funny, anymore. It was time to move little Miss I'm-
Wild to a higher level, get this foolishness over, once and
for all.

Forcing a nonchalance he didn't feel, he challenged
with a grin, "Okay, sweetheart. You want to play
games?" He winked, the brief act geared to taunt and
frighten. "Let's play."

CHAPTER SIX

OLIVIA snapped out of her daydream, embarrassed to realize she'd been having the most outlandish fantasy about Zachary Merit. *Wait a minute, she told herself. You weren't doing anything wrong! Pull yourself together!* A telltale heat scorched her face as she tried to put the man she'd been undressing in her mind out of her thoughts. The fact that she failed miserably made her nervous and she toyed fretfully with a strand of her hair.

Ever since the wig fiasco three hours ago, she'd avoided Zack. He'd been unreasonably brusque. Then he'd made that vague threat. She'd decided to keep to herself as much as possible. Moments ago she'd returned from an aimless stroll over the island. Barefoot. No shoes at all. She'd changed into a cropped tee and shorts, and at the last minute kicked off her sandals, feeling like she was doing something illicit! She'd smirked at that feeling, facing the fact that she had a long way to go in her loosening up. Going without shoes was a far cry from stripping down and running naked into the sea.

She had to admit, though, the freer clothes were starting to grow on her. Even the chance sight of her own belly in a mirror didn't shock her any longer. "Brazen hussy," she murmured with a short, cynical laugh. "That's exactly what Daddy would say." She shook her head at the very idea.

Crossing her legs, she lounged back, watching the incoming waves foam across the beach. The walk had been serene enough—at least the scenery had been serene, though she hadn't been able to find much peace. What had Zack meant by "let's play"? She tried not to read anything sexual into it, but for some demented reason, that was all she'd been able to picture in her head—and it was driving her crazy.

"Liv?"

Zack walked toward Olivia onto the shady loggia. She jumped and twisted around, looking tense and strangely guilty. Good. Why shouldn't she be just as unsettled as he?

"I—is it time for dinner?" She sounded like she was asking if it was time for her firing squad. He pursed his lips, annoyed that he could so easily bring out her run-for-your-life mode. *No, Merit, that's the mode you want to bring out in her, stupid! Get a handle on your libido around this woman!*

"Maybe I'd better go change?" she asked.

He only wished she would. Preferably that boxy linen job she arrived in. "No great rush."

Even as uneasy as she looked, Zack couldn't help but notice how lovely she was, as delicate as rare porcelain. All that flawless, white skin. He was accustomed to California fad-chic and surgically enhanced facsimiles of the real thing, but that didn't mean he'd lost the ability to recognize genuine beauty when it chanced across his path.

And there she sat, long, pale legs wreaking havoc on his mental processes. The sight made him more determined than ever to follow through on his threat—force her to realize just who and what she was—and wasn't— and give himself some breathing room at the same time.

He needed a few hours when they wouldn't be running head-on into each other. Ever since Liv stepped onto

Merit Island he'd struggled to ignore a wild and foolish desire for her. But now he had to admit that even his best efforts were faulty; his hunger grew stronger by the hour. The painful fire in his belly needed quenching, one way or the other. He knew better than to take the easy way, the way he'd always taken. But he wasn't sure how much longer he could fight the good fight and keep winning.

From long years of experience, he'd learned men like him didn't mix with women like Liv, at least not for long. They were like oil and water, fire and ice. He was Mr. Reckless and she, Miss Reliable. Oh, sure, he could be useful briefly as her Wild Weekend Man; but she could be nothing for him but an emotional hangover.

He was trying to move past all that. But where was he headed? And to what? He was floundering and he didn't know when or if he'd ever get his footing.

Liv stood up and twisted to face him, looking cautious but determined. Evidently she expected him to tell her what "let's play" meant, and she clearly didn't expect to like it. But blast her, she also looked like she didn't intend to back down.

Her expression dripped with such tragic bravado, he ached to pull her into his arms and…and…shake some sense into her! At least, that's what he *told* himself he wanted to do. Though he was disturbed that he found her both maddeningly mulish and absurdly adorable, he forced a grin. "It's time we tried something different."

Her fearful, yet resolved stance didn't ease. "Like what? Shaving my head and ramming a safety pin through my cheek?"

"Maybe later."

Her eyes narrowed, exhibiting very clearly she was far from reassured.

Losing his smile, he indicated that she follow him.

Being close to her when she was all fiery and dressed like—*like this*—was wearing him down. He had no energy to trade barbs. He'd used it all up working to keep his hands off her. "Come inside," he grumbled. "Dinner should be soon. After we eat, we'll go."

"Go?" Suspicion chilled her tone.

He had difficulty not wincing at her distrust. This stupid unearth-my-wild-side game was her idea, not his. "You're going to spend a night on Haunted Rock." This object lesson would do them both good. She needed to be scared witless, and he needed her gone. Why, in such a huge mansion, Susan insisted on housing Olivia in the room beside his was a mystery to him. He had a sneaky suspicion there was matchmaking afoot. *Damn that movie!* If he didn't get some time away from Olivia he'd do something foolish they'd both regret.

"Haunted Rock's an islet not far away." He swept an arm toward the sea. "I'll drop you off tonight, then pick you up in the morning. There's nothing like alone-time in dark isolation, for exposing the feral animal in a person." *And it'll give me some alone-time to have a stern talk with myself.*

Counting on her damnable, dogged pluck to work *for* him this time, he challenged grimly, "Are you game?"

Dinner long over, Olivia watched the sun perish in a fiery show. She huddled on the side of her bed, staring out her window, yet not really absorbing the majesty of the sunset. Her mind focused inward as she brooded and worried. She didn't like this latest challenge, but she was determined to throw off her overcivilized lifestyle. She'd had no choice but to agree to spend the night on Haunted Rock.

A knock at her door brought her head up. She sucked in an anxious breath. "Yes?"

"It's time."

Zack made the statement with the tone of an executioner coming for the condemned. Less than enthusiastic, she stood. She didn't like the reluctance in her thinking or the heaviness in her step as she picked up the canvas bag in which she'd packed a few necessities. If she *did* have a wild side still viable enough to be saved—which she wanted badly to be true—she must put aside her qualms and do this thing.

There was nothing dangerous about this trip. She was simply going camping overnight, alone, on a deserted speck of stone in the ocean. Nothing to it. There must be millions of women in the world who would be thrilled by such an adventure.

She swallowed as she trudged to the door, her lug-soled boots dragging along the carpeting. She'd changed into jeans and a scoop-neck cotton sweater that was awfully scanty, but garments three sizes too small were apparently fashionable—though why she felt the need to be fashionable when she was being dumped, all alone, on a pile of ocean-going granite mystified her.

"Liv?"

"I'm coming." She grabbed the crystal knob and swung the door wide.

There he stood, a hunk too handsome for his own good. The sight stole her breath. He wasn't smiling, which was just as well, since the sight of his dimples tended to rattle her. Even unsmiling, he was a sexy devil. He wore jeans and a russet knit shirt, showing off a well-toned, tanned physique that was troubling at best. Under one arm, he carried a bedroll. Apparently she wouldn't have to sleep on the sand after all.

She decided it was a good thing he planned to leave her all alone. She wasn't comfortable with the idea of watching him as he slept in the flickering glow of a campfire. Zack thought she was a neurotic pest anyway, so disgracing herself by jumping him in his sleep would *not* advance her cause. She'd promised him faithfully there would be no touching. What was her problem, lately? She'd never had difficulty keeping her hands off a man before.

"Ready?" he asked, snapping her out of her mental turmoil.

She nodded, mumbling, "I suppose, but if you want my opinion, this seems more stupid than wild."

Though his forehead remained creased in a frown, his lips quirked, displaying those unsettling dimples. "So what's your point, sweetheart?" Grasping her wrist, he hauled her out of the room.

Liv eyed his broad back with a mixture of arousal and resentment. What was that remark supposed to mean? "Are you admitting that a lot of what's labeled 'wild' *is* stupid?" she demanded, stomping up beside him.

He looked at her as they arrived at the head of the grand staircase. With the significant lift of one eyebrow, his expression held a clear "yes".

He tugged her down the stairs. Dashing along in his wake, she grew more and more irked by his disdain of what she was attempting to do, especially considering much of his own life had been lived on the wild side. "Who are you to look down your nose at what I'm trying to do?" she asked. "Just because you've gotten older and—and…" *Wiser* came to mind, but that wasn't the word she was groping for. It would hardly bolster her side of the debate.

"And what?" he coaxed.

She could tell by the twist of his lips he knew she'd thought of "wiser" and she was trying to come up with something more workable.

"Older and *pigheaded*," she blurted.

His laughter was curt. "Me?" He halted, eyeing her with amused skepticism. "You're calling *me* pigheaded?" With the shake of his head, he mouthed something she decided she was better off not catching. "Come on, Wild Thing." He towed her toward the mansion's entry. "Let's get you to Haunted Rock. I have a late date."

She scowled as he hustled her down the front steps and across the manicured lawn. He had a late date? Since when? She felt a stab of—of *something*, and couldn't imagine why. There was no reason to be upset. She wanted to be wild. She wanted to be able to do out-of-the-ordinary things. Camping out without benefit of room service wasn't exactly like trekking through an Amazon marsh writhing with anacondas. The experience would do her good.

She should be exhilarated. After all, she had no claim on Zack. He wasn't her type—even if he liked her, which he didn't. What was her problem with him having a date while she was camping out on a deserted pile of rocks?

"You have a *date*?" She bit her tongue. It sounded like she'd said that out loud. It also sounded like an accusation.

He glanced her way, his expression wary. "So?"

"But—but with *who*?" She cursed herself for not being able to keep her mouth shut.

He slid her a curious look, then grinned. Dimpling in the sunset was very cruel of him. "Whom."

"Huh?"

He drew her up the step onto the dock. "But with

whom.'' He peered at her. "Or is ticking off the grammar police part of the new, wild you?" Without waiting for her response, he indicated the nearest of three moored cruisers. "We've been assigned this one. Watch your step."

"How do you know it's 'whom'?" she asked, finding the leap in subjects bizarre. She'd had a lot of time to lie awake thinking all manner of thoughts about Zachary Merit, but debating grammar hadn't been among them. "Huh, smart guy?" she asked with a smirk. "What makes you so sure it's 'whom'?"

"Get aboard." Jerking his head toward the ladder, he muttered, "I'll untie us."

She jounced up the metal rungs to the cruiser's deck and watched him release the boat. When he joined her onboard, he lounged against the gunwale. "You think I'm too ignorant to know when to use whom, don't you?" he asked, nostrils flaring.

His indictment took her by surprise, and she flinched. "Uh—well—it's just that…"

His jaw muscles bunched. "Right. Sure." Dropping the bedroll on a bench seat, he brushed past her and sat down at the controls. "You'd better park yourself, Miss Nordstrom. The sea's a little rough."

While he fired the engines she took the seat next to his. The instrument panel glowed as the day faded. She peeked at his profile and the dock lights came on in a blinding flash. If she'd had any doubts before, she had none now. Grim was the only word to describe his expression, stark in the flood of fluorescence. She'd insulted his intelligence and that hurt his feelings. Was it possible she had a touch of a superior attitude about her Ivy League education? She'd never thought so, but…

Laying the canvas bag on the deck, she wadded her

hands in her lap. It didn't matter whether she'd blurted the slur as teasing repartee or an unconscious slight brought on by his goading; she'd hurt him. She hadn't meant to, but she did. As Zack began to maneuver away from the dock, she murmured, "I'm sorry."

"What?" he shouted over the engine noise.

She faced him, yelling back, "I said, *I'm sorry.*"

He looked at her. "What for?"

"For the *whom* thing," she called. "What else?"

He eyed heaven then returned his attention to the choppy sea.

"I didn't mean to belittle you."

"Yes, you did."

She frowned, her repentance mutating into animosity. "No, I did *not!* And I've apologized, so can we get back to who you have this alleged date with? And don't try to change the subject by tossing back *'with whom you have this date,'* buddy, because the grammar-evasion tactic only works once."

"You don't know her," he shouted.

"I'm sure I don't. So what's her name and where did you meet her?"

"Mary Louise—something." He altered their course slightly but didn't look at her. "I've never met the woman, and Marc fixed us up."

"Is she coming to the island?" Olivia couldn't imagine why she needed the details. But for some reason she did.

"I'm meeting her in Portland." He shifted the boat into cruising speed.

"In Portland?" she asked, surprised. "Aren't you afraid you'll be recognized and harassed?"

He gave her the oddest look. It almost seemed as though he were saying, *Harassed worse than you?* Finally he shook his head. "I'll risk it."

They bounced over the waves, the experience both exhilarating and disagreeable—very much like her churlish companion. "That really will make it a late date," she yelled, shocked to find she needed to say *that*, of all things.

He peered at her. "I'm a big boy. I don't have a curfew."

She broke eye contact. Her stomach began to churn and she swallowed hard. "What—what if there's an emergency?" she shouted.

"What are you talking about?"

She faced him, affronted. He could certainly put her out of his mind with great dispatch. "What if I fall down and break a leg? How will I let you know?"

His eyebrows dipped. "Don't fall down and break a leg."

She stared, her lips gaping. *What kind of a slipshod plan was this?*

His lips twisted with sardonic amusement. "I wish you could see your expression," he said. "It's not the face of a woman about to burst into full-blown wildness. It's the face of a frightened little girl who wants Daddy."

Any seasickness she might have given in to under normal circumstances was overwhelmed by sudden, stinging resentment. She clamped her jaws so quickly she almost fractured some back teeth.

Silently she vowed morning would find her whole and well and successful in her assault on her Charm School outershell. By tomorrow, there would be fissures in it, maybe even a gaping hole.

She spun to stare straight ahead, opting not to look into his eyes. "You only *wish* I'm a frightened little girl, Mr. Merit," she grumbled. "Go on your date. I'll be fine!"

CHAPTER SEVEN

BY THE time Zack deposited Liv onshore with a sleeping bag and her sack of supplies, she didn't think Haunted Rock looked so scary. The island was nothing more than a hill of boulders surrounded by sandy beach, scrubby trees and bushes, and here and there a spotty patch of sea grass. This would be a snap. She'd spread out her sleeping bag and watch the stars until she fell asleep. Before she knew it, the sun would be up and Zack would be back.

Zack would be back! She chewed the inside of her cheek as he climbed aboard the cruiser and headed for the controls. She watched him from shore, feeling abandoned—physically and emotionally. Why was that? Just because he was leaving her alone in the middle of nowhere to go on a date with some—some *woman*—was no reason to feel forsaken. She must *not* let it hurt to watch him matter-of-factly sail away, his hot date the only thing on his mind.

Promising herself this night would help prove she was a woman who could kick life in the teeth and laugh, she made herself turn away. Hefting the sleeping bag under one arm, she grabbed up the canvas sack. The cruiser's engine sparked to life, and her heart lurched.

The rumble died. An eerie stillness filled the night.

The engine coughed to life again, then died. This time the quiet was deafening.

Cough—silence.

Confused, she looked back. In the dead stillness, she called out. "What are you doing?"

She could see his face in the greenish glow of the control panel. He didn't look happy.

Cough—silence.

Cough—silence.

Cough—silence.

Liv was beginning to detect a pattern. She might not be a genius with motors, but she sensed something was wrong. Depositing her gear on the sand, she walked to the water's edge. Since she was barefoot and her jeans were wet almost to her hips from wading ashore, she sloshed out to the ladder and clambered aboard. Padding to the cockpit, she leaned against the leather seat she'd occupied, and peered at Zack.

Cough—silence.

He turned the key again. This time she heard nothing but a weak *click...click...click.*

"Damn," he gritted out.

"Anything wrong?"

He eyed her with aggravation. "No. Everything's dandy. The engines are purring like kittens. Can't you hear them?"

She made a face at his sarcasm, not sure why she was more pleased than worried. Conceivably the idea of Zack not making his midnight rendezvous with Mata Hari, or whatever her name was, had something to do with it, but she repressed that notion. "It sounds like you have a dead battery."

He shifted to stare at her. "Oh? You're not only a financial whiz and a grammar scholar, but you're also a mechanic?"

She scowled at him. "I took a course in high school called Lady, Know Your Car. If boat batteries aren't a lot different than car batteries, then that's what a dead battery sounds like.''

"Mmm." His nod was mocking. "As the expert, what would you suggest?"

She shrugged. "Well, if we had another boat, we could—"

"We don't. What else?" He sounded more instructive than curious.

"Uh, buy new batteries?"

An eyebrow rose, indicating the potential for finding battery stores nearby was not good.

Appalled to realize she felt more pleased than unsettled to think he might not be able to leave, she leaned down, frowning. "I thought you were a racing boat guru. Don't you know what to do?"

He glowered at the control panel, now dark. "I guess the batteries were low when the boat was plugged into shore power," he muttered. "The converter kept it charged enough to get the engines started, but while they were shut down just now, it's a safe bet the refrigerator sucked out the last of the juice."

"What about calling for help?"

He shook his head. "Radio won't work without battery power."

"Oh—right." She struggled with her conscience for a few seconds. She didn't want him to go on a date. Didn't want him to abandon her. On the other hand, nothing good would come from spending the night with him. She didn't like to admit it, but being alone with Zack was dangerous, and she'd already made a fool of herself around him. "Uh, I brought a cell phone—for emergencies," she mumbled. "I'll go get it."

He glanced up sharply, but didn't speak. She couldn't tell if he was pleased by this stroke of luck or provoked at her inability to leave her phone on the island. Was his silence pleasant shock, or was he merely resisting telling her this was another example of her total inability to cast off her dependence on modern conveniences?

Before he changed his mind and decided to voice his condemnation, she hurried away, waded to shore and plucked her phone from the canvas bag. Hustling back onboard, she dialed the island's security number. It didn't take long to find out the cell phone was about as useful as a banana for communication. "I guess we're in a dead spot," she admitted, at last. "I can't reach anybody."

"Typical." He slouched back. "Looks like I won't be going to Portland tonight."

"That's a shame." She tried to mean it. But her relief at knowing Zack would miss his tryst with little Miss Hot-Body-Something made actual distress difficult to pull off.

He shifted toward her. "Yeah, I see you're crushed." He stood. "If you don't mind, I think I'll go check the engines. I'm sure I'll be able to fix it." He grabbed a flashlight from where it was stored beneath the dashboard. Brushing past her, he muttered, "I *damn* well better be able to."

She breathed in his pleasing scent and shifted to stare after him as he headed aft. Feeling ridiculously buoyant, she lounged against the seat. It was dark, with only the full moon and the beam of his flashlight to banish the blackness. Resting her elbows on the chair-back, she fought a wayward grin. "No nookie for you tonight, Mr. Merit? I'm so sorry for you."

Her remark seemed overly loud, fairly bouncing off the water, echoing off rocks and ricocheting around the boat. She flinched as her gibe came back to bellow at her from all sides. Luckily Zack had gone below so he couldn't have overheard. Even so she was upset with herself. What was she thinking? She didn't want Zack marooned out here on this little speck of land with her? Did she?

She experienced a crazy fluttering in her chest. Oh, how she wished she didn't want it. Hadn't she just reminded herself of her "no touching" pledge? But what was the use in kidding herself? Deep down in her foolish, palpitating heart, Liv knew there was nothing on earth she wanted more.

How could this have happened? With all the mechanical and security employees on Merit Island, how did Zack end up with a cruiser that could only be used as a doorstop? Fuming and muttering, he lay on his back in the bunk, below deck. Why had he told Marc to tell Mary Louise he'd "make it if he could"? Why had he left it that she should go out with a group of her friends to a local club, and he'd show up "when" and "if"?

Okay, so at first he'd had a few qualms about paparazzi. Later, he'd decided it was worth the gamble, to indulge in a little—ahem—female companionship. He was restless and irritable, had been for days. He needed to relax and let go. He knew the cure for that would be a romp with some uncomplicated female who would *not* one day live in the White House and would *not* go into the history books as the "beautiful and brilliant First Daughter."

But, *no*. The Fates got their pointy heads together and decided to body-slam him into Olivia *again*! What kind of a hellish penance were they putting him through, and why? Was it to atone for his self-indulgent, reckless lifestyle over the years? Is that why the blasted boat had to go stone-cold dead?

If so, the Fates were a fiendish lot, toying with his life—making it work out that Marc expected Zack to be in Portland all night, and Mary Louise knew not to count on him. In other words, *nobody* would check on his whereabouts until he—and Liv—didn't show up for lunch tomorrow.

Tomorrow.

Blast it! Of all the lousy luck, *this* had to take the prize. Somewhere not far away, on the other side of a few paltry rocks, Olivia Nordstrom was sleeping—or more likely huddled in a frightened ball, petrified of every murmur of surf, rustle of leaves or shriek of a seabird. He closed his eyes to shut out the vision, but it wouldn't go away.

He had a gut feeling she had no intention of giving in to fear. She'd stick it out even if the alleged ghost of Haunted Rock showed up and spooked the life out of her. He and his brothers had camped here as kids. They'd never seen the ghost, and Zack didn't believe in such silliness, but who knew what Liv might conjure up in her fright. What if she thought she saw the specter? What if she panicked and bolted into the sea?

He sat up, a chill of foreboding skidding down his spine. "Who would you blame if that happened, jackass?" he growled.

Swinging his legs to the floor, he grabbed his jeans and yanked them on. In another minute he was loping noiselessly along the beach. He hoped his fears were unfounded and she was asleep, but he had to check. He would never forgive himself if his desire to teach her a lesson, and get her out of his reach for a few hours, caused her harm.

He heard a high-pitched squeal and stopped. Crouching behind low scrub, he searched the dimness. That cry had definitely not been a bird. Since he had excellent night vision, the full moon was illumination enough for him to spot her sleeping bag. He peered at it. Wadded queerly, it didn't look as though a person could possibly be inside.

Another squeal and a flash of movement caught his eye. He scanned the blackness beyond the beach, detecting movement again. Something was out there, in the surf. Something pale and—and...

"Naked," he murmured.

He stared in a state of paralysis. Was that gorgeous sprite Liv? That pale, shapely phantom splashing and playing in the water—could it be...

He swallowed, his throat parched. "Oh, fine," he croaked, closing his eyes and sinking back to sit on the sand. He felt a little afflicted at the moment. Afflicted by an attack of lust. Wincing, he rolled to his back. The sand held residual warmth from the sun, but it couldn't compare with the heat that singed his flesh and scorched his belly.

"No," he groaned. "You do not love that woman. Don't even think it." To her, he was an ignorant muscle-brain, an inept one, at that, considering even with all his so-called expertise about boats he couldn't fix the cruiser. Hell, he wasn't a magician. He couldn't conjure up batteries out of thin air. He heaved a sigh. Right now, with his gut torqued in painful knots, he'd give an arm and both legs for that ability.

Draping his forearm over his eyes, he struggled to will himself into another state of mind. A state that didn't debilitate him to the point of leaving him prostrate in the sand, moaning.

He heard a distant giggle and visions of her pale femininity loomed in his mind. He groaned and rolled to his side, pushing up on one elbow. "Get a grip, man," he warned, under his breath. Unfortunately for him, he happened to roll into a position that allowed him a clear view of her, flouncing and bouncing in the surf.

Muttering a colorful earful to the Fates, he shoved himself up on one knee. With Herculean effort, he stood—hunched and hurting—his fondest hope to stagger into the darkness and die.

A flicker of movement in the night made Liv instinctively drop to her knees in the surf. She went still and peered into the darkness where she'd seen—something. What was it—lumbering erratically out of sight. She'd only spotted it a half-second before it disappeared behind rocks.

A wave hit her, knocking her forward. She righted herself and swept water from her stinging eyes. Her heart began to pound as terrifying scenarios began to parade before her mind's eye. Somebody—or something—was on this island besides her. Well, there was Zack, of course, but she knew Zack's walk, and that wasn't it.

Could it have been the island's ghost out for a fitful haunt? She shuddered, hugging herself. The water was too cold for malingering and cowering. Besides, she didn't believe in ghosts. Biting her lip, she tried to work out her options. Her clothes were folded neatly on a tuft of grass, but the bedroll was closer.

Deciding speed was her ally, she dashed from the surf and in three seconds had the bedding wrapped around her. Her only thought was to get to the cruiser. Zack was there. If the entity she'd spied was more human and lethal than a spook, she wanted to be somewhere *inside* with someone else—and it didn't hurt if that someone was six and a half feet tall and over two hundred pounds of solid, sexy muscle.

If she hadn't been so frightened, she might have worked on amending her description, canceling "sexy," but she couldn't worry about that now. She needed to concentrate on *not* being captured and devoured or deflowered or de-whatever deranged castaways did to idiot females they found running around naked.

Swaddled in the sleeping bag, she galloped over the sand at a good clip, considering her nonaerodynamic ensemble. Bunching the bag around her, she splashed out to the boat and scrambled aboard, half-inclined to throw off the bedding for a quicker ascent. But some part of her brain clung to the rules of modesty drilled into her over the years, so she held onto the bedroll.

When she charged down the steps below deck, Zack was seated on his bunk, looking toward the hatch. Of course her noisy approach would have disturbed his sleep. He opened his mouth to speak, but she dashed into his arms, hanging on for dear life. "Zack," she cried, out of breath, "Somebody was out there—watching me."

His arms came around her. She sensed his hesitancy but wouldn't be put off. She'd been frightened out of her wits, and it would take some time in the refuge of his embrace before her panic ebbed.

"Uh—" He cleared his throat. "Don't—"

"I know," she cut in. "Please don't say it. I know I shouldn't be here. I know I was probably just seeing things. Please don't tell me a wild woman wouldn't give in to her fears. I *know* all that—"

"*Shut up*, Liv," he growled near her ear.

Stunned by his vehemence, she leaned away to look into his face. It was extraordinary how moonlight spilling through the hatch illuminated his features, as though heaven was making a point to spotlight him. Of all the worthy things on earth, Zack Merit had been sought out by meandering moonbeams for the scrutiny of the gods. And not without reason. He was a stirring vision. His chiseled features were tender, yet troubled. She was both enthralled and unsettled by what she saw.

She had no idea why, but an all-powerful need surged over her. Vow or no vow, she suddenly knew it was right to give herself to this man—body and soul. More alive than she'd ever felt, she kissed him. The heady intimacy, the sense of being where she was meant to be, set her heart thundering.

Ever since the day Zachary Merit rescued her, she'd known, but wouldn't allow herself to see—until now. She'd fallen in love with him, and no amount of reasoning with herself about the inappropriateness of their match would help.

Zack was the man—the *only* man—to lead her from her shell and transform her into a living, breathing woman.

Zack struggled to resist the damnable sweetness of Liv's kiss. Her sleeping bag drooped off one shoulder, baring much of her slender back. He tried to ignore the velvet texture of her skin, tried not to caress the undraped flesh. But hot slivers of desire ripped through his belly and his fingers ached to fondle and inflame.

Her lips coaxed and teased, goaded and dared. His resistance faltered. Sweat beaded his brow. Ever since their first kiss, he'd fought a nagging urgency to hold her this way, to relish the feel, the scent, the smoothness and tang of her skin and her mouth. But he knew the downside of wild abandon, and he sensed that indulging with the senator's heaven-born princess would be harder on him than any of the fling-seeking *glitterati* who had come before.

She opened her lips, her kiss deepening as she pressed

her body into his. The bedroll slipped further and he felt soft, yielding flesh against his chest. The contact so overwhelmed him he inhaled sharply. A low moan filled the quiet and he realized it had come from the depth of his embattled soul.

Damnation, Merit! Stop this before it goes too far! he warned. Yet even as he admonished himself, his lips parted, and he reveled in the deep kiss they shared. Behind closed eyelids, he saw fireworks rivaling anything a world of millennium celebrations could boast.

Her lips, her tongue, her body pressed intimately into his, throbbed a passionate message, an ardent plea to be taken, shamelessly and completely. He knew the signs. He also knew one day she would go back to her society balls where the cream of Park Avenue, Beacon Hill and the White House schemed and schmoozed.

Right now she wasn't thinking beyond tonight, but he couldn't afford not to. This woman was different. Not in what she wanted from him, but in the way she made him feel—elated and whole, yet unworthy and defenseless. He didn't like the crazy mix of emotions, and was afraid knowing her physically and passionately would leave him with a wound that would never heal.

He couldn't picture the likes of him on her arm, attending some gala society ball. The president's dazzling daughter and a rebel dropout careening toward middle age, with nothing to show for his life but a list of things he could drive fast. Unfortunately for them both, Liv was bound and determined to be added to that list. Tonight.

Zack tried to remain focused, to remember that once she regained her sanity, and lost interest in uncovering her adventurous side, she'd understand any match between them was as laughable as taking a baboon into a luxurious Manhattan condo.

She lifted her mouth away from his and buried her face in his neck, dropping hot kisses along his throat. He stilled, unable to move or think, as her lips burned his flesh like a dream come true. Nipping at his earlobe, she cried breathlessly, "Make love to me, Zachary."

Her tongue darted into his ear, the act so flagrantly erotic it could drive a marble statue into lewd and unstatuelike behavior. The sad fact was, Zack wasn't made of marble. His mangled resolve teetered on the edge of oblivion. With a last, desperate bid for self-preservation, he slid his hands from the bliss of her back. Gripping her arms, he pressed her away.

"*I* was the shadow that frightened you," he ground out, working to make her detest him and stomp away, for this small separation was all he could manage. He could no more walk right now than he could fly. "*I* was the degenerate ogling you from the bushes." His throat closed with need. Unable to speak, he could only stare, a mute witness, as her expression changed from ardent to disconcerted to horrified.

"What?" Her question came out high-pitched with disbelief.

He swallowed. No longer able to look at her face, he dropped his gaze. Not a good move, since her bare breasts came into view. Feeling like his gut was being crushed in a vise, he shifted to stare into the blackness over her shoulder. He fumbled with the bedroll, covering her. "I said," he whispered hoarsely, "I was the one sneaking around watching you."

She gasped, and he knew she finally understood the ugly picture he painted. Though it wasn't a totally accurate picture, it was necessary. As his coup de grâce, he twisted his lips into a sneer. "Get it through your head,

Miss Nordstrom,'' he warned. ''Wild things attract predators.''

Her eyes went wide. A heartbeat later she wrenched from his grip with a shuddery cry. He braced for the sting of her slap but it didn't come. Instead she stumbled up the steps to the deck. Without turning, he peered toward the exit to see the tail of her bedroll disappear. Closing his eyes, he listened as she tromped to the ladder and clambered down. Then there was nothing but silence.

He didn't know how long he sat there before he finally sucked in a breath. Slumping forward he held his head in his hands. He didn't feel well. Until this moment he'd never known what pure sexual frustration felt like. Considering the crushing throb in his belly, he wasn't sure if this torture was preferable to being used by Liv Nordstrom and then discarded. Even so, something lurking around the edges of his heart told him *this* choice was the most bearable.

''How in blazes…?'' He expelled a rough groan and rolled to his back, experiencing a wretchedness he'd never known possible. For the remainder of the night, Zachary stared unseeing into the darkness, gritting his teeth against the pain.

CHAPTER EIGHT

Liv had never been so humiliated in her life. How many times did she have to be rejected by a man before she got the message that he didn't want anything to do with her? Evidently in Zack's case, once hadn't been enough. She vowed by every grain of sand on the beach, the next time she jumped Zachary Merit it would be for nothing *less* satisfying than to strangle him.

She hunched on the shore, staring out to sea. From the location of the sun Liv had no idea what time it was. Maybe nine, or eight, possibly ten. In her rat race of a job, she didn't get much chance to see the sun, let alone tell time by it. Hours before dawn she'd eaten the one meal she'd brought, a peanut butter sandwich and an apple. All she had left was a quart of tepid water, which wasn't particularly filling.

She'd been anxious at dinner last night and had hardly swallowed a bite. If she weren't so furious and insulted and mortified right now, she would be starving. As things stood, she just felt mad—mainly at herself. How could she have acted like such a fool last night?

She hadn't seen Zack, today, which was a blessing. She supposed he was hiding out, afraid she'd leap on him again and beg him to—

With a choked moan she covered her face, angry with herself that his rejection hurt so much. She needed to get a grip so she could face him unflinching, with her shoulders back. Show him his disinterest had precious little effect on her. *"Ha!"* she said without inflection. ''I'll show you how much your rejection bothered me, you—you—''

"Dirtbag?"

She jerked around to spot the last person in the galaxy she cared to find. *He* stood there, half nude. A mean-spirited thing to do, considering her mental state. His upper torso glistened and his jeans were soaked and clung to him. She swallowed with difficulty, finding it hard to blame the jeans for their possessiveness. What anatomy she could detect through the sodden denim was certainly—

Forcing her attention to his face, she cleared her throat, irked with herself for her turn of mind. "Dirtbag?" She pushed up to stand and jutted her chin. "I see you've spent the night productively—reaching sound conclusions about your character."

He glared, a sign her insult stung. Shoving a hand through his hair, he scattered sun-gilded drops in the breeze. Belatedly she noticed he sported a tattoo. A double band design that mimicked barbed wire stretched around his muscle-hardened upper arm. Making matters worse, he had one of those confounded California tans. His skin glistened from his swim, highlighting every bulge and plane of bronze flesh, as though he'd been oiled down for a photo shoot.

Why did he have to look like an advertisement for macho-man motorcycles? Or—or one of those late-night, nine-hundred number commercials where some buff-and-shirtless hunk grins into the camera and invites in a husky come-on, "Call me, sugar, and I'll talk dirty to you."

She had a feeling if he made that suggestion on camera, the phone system in North America would be tied up for months. But as far as Zack ever saying it to her—fat chance! He barely talked to her, let alone…

She bit her tongue as punishment for allowing such thoughts to creep into her brain. Sucking in a breath, she decided to be as big a pain as he was. "Is that little doodad your only tattoo?" she asked, waving offhandedly.

His eyebrows dipped but his lips crooked in a grin. She didn't like the combination. It was almost as though he was asking, "And just how many tattoos do you have?" Why could he make her feel like a fool without opening his mouth? Her cheeks began to burn at the memory of his mouth—last night—and how his kiss had coaxed and thrilled, and how...

She bit down on her tongue again. *Do not think about that!* She stared him down trying not to think about anything. She wanted to look away, but knew she had to show him she was absolutely fine with his rejection, even if she wasn't.

"So—where do you hide all your other tattoos?" she asked, then flinched. *What kind of a stupid question was that? Did she want him to show her?* Fighting a rush of desire, she tried for disdain in her expression and flippancy in her tone. "If you have one on your *gluteus maximus* that says Kick Me, it's a shame you keep it covered."

She heard it, but she had a hard time believing it. *It's a shame you keep it covered? Had she said that out loud? Olivia Nordstrom, have you donated your mind to charity?* She shuddered at the magnitude of her Freudian blunder.

He grinned, but the expression didn't reach his eyes. At least she didn't think so, since they were narrowed. "To answer your question, I don't have any more tattoos, but I'll keep your gluteus maximus suggestion in mind."

He inhaled. She knew that because of the unforgivable

way her glance was snagged by gleaming pectoral muscles when his chest expanded.

"Hungry?" he asked.

She frowned for a heartbeat before she cast her gaze down. "No," she murmured, examining her fingernails. He was too good-looking, and that troubled her beyond bearing.

"Come on, Liv," he urged, sounding doubtful. "You fainted that first night you were here because you let yourself get run down. You need food."

She glared at him. "Maybe, but what do you suggest I eat? Sand?" She had a thought and hope billowed. "Or was there some food in that refrigerator that sucked out the last of the battery's juice?"

"A couple of dill pickle slices." He folded his arms over his chest. "I ate them for breakfast."

Her hope died a quiet death. "Two whole slices? And you ate them both? What a pig." She was kidding, but she didn't feel like smiling.

He watched her for a pulse beat, then shook his head. "Have you tried calling out for a pizza?"

She eyed him with affront. "I love a good joke. Keep talking. Maybe the next one will be good."

He smirked. "When the industrial revolution fails us, Miss Nordstrom, we're driven to fend for ourselves." He grasped her arm and tugged her along the shoreline.

"Where are you taking me?" She jerked on his hold but couldn't pull free.

"To your first fending lesson." He indicated a scrubby tree that looked dead. "First we build a fire." He pulled something from his hip pocket and with a flick of his wrist a steel blade appeared. It was the most lethal Swiss Army knife she'd ever seen. "I'm thinking fresh fish, limpets, sea urchin gonads, with a side of sugarwrack. How does that sound?''

"Did you say something about gonads?'' she asked, confused.

He let her go and expertly separated a dead branch from a tree trunk. "Here.'' He thrust the firewood at her. "You carry.''

"Gee, thanks, Tarzan.'' For a long moment she stared at the back of his head, worrying her lower lip. "But aren't gonads—''

"Yes, they are.'' He piled another branch on the first and peered at her. "And they're eaten raw.'' His lips quirked. "They're not Pig's trotters hash, but they're damn fine eating. Especially if you're hungry.''

She made a face. "I could never get that hungry.''

"Yes, you could.'' He broke off another branch and added it to the growing pile. "I've no idea what time we'll be rescued, and in a few hours you'll be ready to eat anything.''

"Not raw gonads.''

"And raw seaweed, which you'll harvest.''

"Me?'' Weighed down with deadwood, her voice showed the strain.

"Or I could gather the seaweed while you catch the fish.''

"Catch them doing what?''

He closed one eye in an exaggerated wince. "That old joke just keeps on getting funnier.'' Shaking his head as though she were a hopeless case, he said, "Catch them to *eat* them, Miss Nordstrom.''

She stared at him. "Catch fish with what, my bare hands?''

"That's right.'' He indicated the beach behind her. "Take the wood over there. It looks like a good spot.''

"Are you nuts? Who catches fish bare-handed?"

Kneeling, he'd begun to whack at the scrawny tree trunk. His knife flashed in the sun. "I do. Unless you'd rather. But I warn you, it takes practice. You might be very hungry by the time you catch anything."

"Or very dead from old age."

He didn't immediately respond. His knife continued to flash as he cut. "While I build the fire you collect the limpets. You'll need the knife."

"I'm not stabbing anything!"

He stood and gave the trunk a hearty push. It cracked and fell to the sand with a dull thud. Employing a quick twist of his arm, he separated the downed trunk from the remainder of its bark and hefted it. Luscious muscle bulged all over his glistening torso, sending Olivia's pulse into a frothy jig.

"They have to be pried off rocks," he said. "Limpets are called the poor man's escargot and they're good emergency survival food."

Tugging her gaze from his taut flesh, she wrinkled her nose with distaste. "I'd rather eat sand."

His chuckle was cynical. "Unless you have a gizzard, I wouldn't recommend it."

With a wave, he indicated the nearby inlet containing a tranquil tidal pool. "We'll lay out the fire, then I'll show you what a limpet looks like and how to find the most tender fronds of *Laminaria sacarina*." He glanced her way. "You still have some fresh water, right?"

She readjusted the firewood in her arms. "Yes. Why?"

"We'll need a little when we clean the fish."

"We?" She was horrified. "You mean the *royal* me? Meaning *you*?"

He lay aside the tree trunk and gave her a quick, penetrating look. "No, I meant we, as in you and me." He took the firewood from her arms. Dropping to one knee, he began to arrange the wood for their campfire. "But, if you don't want my help, you're welcome to do it alone."

"That's not what I meant, and you know it!"

He glanced at her, squinting into the morning sun. "Miss Nordstrom, do I detect a lack of enthusiasm?" Before she could respond, he stood to tower over her. Fisting his hands on his hips, he scowled. "Look, I can do everything by myself. I can fetch and serve, and bow and scrape, and genuflect to your little heart's desire. And after I do, you *will* eat everything, because you need it. And, when it's all said and done and we're off this rock, you'll damn well admit you are not now, and never will be, a wild child. Also, you'll shut up about it for the rest of your stay." He held out a hand. "Do we have a deal?"

She was stunned by his fierceness. It struck her that he'd been leading up to his speech since he'd appeared this morning. Perhaps he was taking a bit of revenge for last night. *He needed revenge?* Her passionate assault on him was so offensive *he* needed revenge?

Resentment and humiliation surged to the surface and she flushed miserably. "We do not have a deal, Mr. Merit!" she said. "Give me that stupid knife and show me the linnets!"

"Linnets are birds, Miss Nordstrom, limpets are mollusks, cousins of the abalone."

"I don't care if they're twins separated at birth from a party hat." She thrust out her hand. "Give me that knife, *Mr.* Merit!"

He seemed startled and glowered at her for several strain-filled seconds. She almost felt like smiling. She liked the notion she'd yanked his smug, know-it-all rug out from under him.

After a minute, he pursed his lips and flipped the knife, catching it deftly by the flat of the blade, to present her with its handle. "Don't hurt yourself."

She grasped it. "Just show me the limpets and get out of my way."

Indicating her feet, he said, "You'd better take off your shoes. You'll be wading in fairly deep water." He met her gaze. "You might want to take off the jeans, too."

"What a great idea." She sat down and lay the knife aside. "And you might want to hold your breath till pigs fly."

"It was just a suggestion."

She tugged off her boots and socks then rolled up her pant legs. "Forget it." Plucking up the knife, she stood. "Let's get on with the fending lesson."

During the next half hour, Zack pointed out the inch long "Chinaman's hat" mollusks called limpets. Patiently and gravely, he explained that moving quietly was essential, because when alerted to danger they tended to cling tight. He demonstrated how to slip the knife under the foot and pry them off rocks. He also showed her how to identify long, flat, yellow-brown fronds of sugarwrack seaweed. He didn't treat her like a second-grader, but she felt like one. She might be an honors graduate from Yale, but this was a whole new kind of education for her, and she was a rank beginner.

Twenty-four hours ago Olivia wouldn't have guessed she would ever possess any fending facts at all. Today, she wasn't sure she was thrilled she did. She was also far from thrilled about Zachary's distant attitude as he gave her instructions. They brushed against each other occasionally, but Olivia had the impression he silently cursed each accidental touch.

She knew Zack was annoyed with every wimpy, whiny, weak-willed fiber of her being. He couldn't have made it more plain if he'd printed it across his chest. She vowed she'd die before she would whimper or complain or cower, no matter what he threw her way. If he told her to bite the head off a snake, she'd do it! She was ashamed of so much of what she'd done lately and how she'd behaved, she swore she wouldn't be a burden or nuisance to him for the rest of their captivity on Haunted Rock.

Now that he'd left her on her own, she haltingly waded around in hip-deep water, scanning the rocky outcroppings, stalking what would later become lunch. She dragged her cinched canvas bag along on one arm, allowing it to be swamped by ocean water. Each limpet she captured went into the partly submerged pouch, because Zack had said mollusks needed to be left in seawater for at least thirty minutes to clean themselves before they were cooked. Olivia planned to make sure the little guys had plenty of time to complete their cleansing regimen. The thought of putting dirty denizens of the deep in her mouth didn't do a thing for her appetite, no matter how hungry she was.

She spied a limpet and readied her knife. Something slithered between her legs and she jumped and shrieked. An instant later she realized nothing was attacking her. It had merely been a blade of seaweed brushing against her calf.

"What happened?" Zack called.

She flicked her glance his way, embarrassed that he'd witnessed another bout of wimpiness. He'd knelt to lay more branches on the growing pile. Stock-still, with an armload of sticks, he looked like a picture postcard for the perfect sun-kissed fantasy-man any right-thinking woman would pick for her stranded-on-a-desert-isle day-dreams. Olivia waved off his concern. ''A poisonous sea snake tried to bite me, but I scared it away,'' she improvised. ''They hate screaming.''

Even from twenty feet away, she could see the questioning quirk of his brow. After a second, he drew his lips in thoughtfully and nodded, looking almost as though he took her ridiculous lie seriously. ''Quick thinking.'' He stood and pivoted away. She flicked her gaze down at the thoroughly forewarned limpet. The last thing she needed to do was admire the way Zack's muscles flexed in his back and arms. Not to mention the taut, sexy curve of his posterior.

She made a face at the mollusk. ''Are you going to give me trouble, too?'' She wedged the knife blade under its foot and lifted, but it stuck tight. ''You must be a male,'' she grumbled.

Olivia was dismayed to find herself eyeing Zack several times as he waded around snagging sea urchins. She also took quiet, curious notice as he gathered flat rocks and a soggy pile of seaweed.

One of the major things she'd noticed during the past hour was that he *didn't* look at her. ''Oh, shut up!'' she muttered.

''Did you say something to me?''

His question from not far away startled her so badly she teetered backward, but caught herself before she fell. After regaining her equilibrium, she peered at him. He stood ten feet away on the beach. ''No, I was talking to Ursula here.'' She held up a limpet she'd just pried free. ''Private stuff. Do you mind?''

He frowned, clearly noting her edginess. Why did he have to affect her so strongly she couldn't control her emotions?

"Have you harvested the seaweed?"

"Yes, sir!" She tossed off a jaunty salute. "As ordered, it's rinsing in the plastic bag my sandwich was in, sir."

"Good. Tie the canvas sack someplace then start the fire." He indicated a rocky peninsula not far away. "I'm going fishing. Don't go over there."

She glanced at the outcropping then back at him. "Bare-handed?"

He spread his arms, really shabby behavior, considering how much time she'd spent trying not to stare at his chest. "If you'll notice, I'm fresh out of fishing gear."

"But I want to watch." She winced. *Was that whining she heard coming from her mouth?*

Zack loped off, shouting, "Start the fire."

"You're pretty sure of yourself, aren't you?"

He reached the finger of rock and turned back. For an instant she thought she saw distress flash across his face but too quickly the illusion disappeared. "Just start the fire."

"What with?"

"I left a waterproof package of matches over there. Figure it out."

Annoyed, she slipped the canvas bag's strap off her arm and wrapped it around a lump of granite to dangle in the surf. "I'm not sure how much loosening up I'm doing," she muttered, "but I'm sure I'll earn my Stuck-In-The-Wilderness-With-A-Grouch merit badge." She stilled, realizing with some irony she'd said *merit* badge. Merit, as in Zachary. "Scary."

She glanced his way. He was lying on his stomach, one arm poised over the water. She stood there watching for a long minute. He didn't move. Not a hair. She shook her head and climbed out of the water to do as Zack had ordered.

Fifteen minutes later, she was bored with fanning the flames. The fire was doing fine. She sat beside it, her arms curled around her knees. With mixed emotions, she cast a glance at Zack. He still lay on his belly looking like a statue. How could he hold himself that still for that long? His muscles must be killing him. She couldn't sit the way she was for more than a few minutes without having to wriggle around to get comfortable.

Tired of tending a fire that didn't need tending, she pushed up and ambled along the beach. The sand between her toes felt good. The sun on her face felt good. Besides the fact that her stomach was growling like a grizzly, she felt awfully good.

After a time, she faced the fact she was ambling toward Zack, but she told herself it didn't mean a thing. She didn't plan to bother him. For a few more minutes, she walked around eyeing him grudgingly as she aimlessly kicked at the sand. She pivoted toward the rock jetty, some foolish, unthinking imp taking dominion over her good sense. "You know, Zack, I wouldn't call this little nature picnic very wild."

"Hush."

She clamped her jaws shut but she didn't stop walking. Very cautiously she edged onto the rocky spur. When she got near enough to Zack that she thought fish might be able to see her, she crouched, crab-walking on her hands and feet silently up beside him.

"I thought I told you to stay away," he whispered, his back to her.

"I want to do that."

"Do it somewhere else."

"I can't if I don't know how."

"Keep your voice down."

She pulled her lower lip between her teeth and lay down on her stomach beside him. Their arms rubbed, but she didn't move away. "I can't do that if I don't know how," she repeated in a low whisper.

He didn't respond, didn't turn, didn't react in any way.

She gritted her teeth. After an eternity of being ignored, she stacked her hands and lay her cheek on them, watching him. Since his attention was riveted on the undulating ocean, she looked him up and down without fear of being caught.

She took in his tempting, sun-bronzed physique, witnessing the coiled power in every muscle, tightly controlled and ready to strike.

Against her will, her femininity reacted strongly to his masculinity. She wanted to stroke that broad, tempting back he presented to her. She wanted to inch closer and sniff his nape. It was a crazy urge—sniffing the man's neck. No, she didn't just want to sniff, she wanted to lick and kiss and nuzzle. The impulse was wild and real. The magnetic pull of his maleness tore at her resistance and a sense of tingling need began to flow over her. Unable to help herself, she lifted her head, inching closer.

"What are you doing?" he asked.

She stopped dead. *What was she doing?* "Nothing!" Olivia was grateful she was fibbing to the back of his head. Her rabid blush would have given her away.

"Look, Liv," he said, his tone low and tight. "This is hard enough without…" He exhaled. "Just be still."

She pulled back, ashamed of her weakness. The man had a will of iron and she had a will of mush. Deciding she needed to get her mind on the business at hand and off nibbling his nape, she asked quietly, "How did you learn to fish like this?"

"From an old Hawaiian."

"No kidding?"

"Aia a kau ka I'ai ka wa'a, mana'o ke ola."

"What?" Panic rushed through her. Was the disconcerting effect of his nearness messing with her hearing? She hadn't understood a word he'd said.

"It's Hawaiian for, 'One can think of life after the fish is in the canoe.'"

She absorbed that and opened her mouth to comment.

"Basically it means shut up until I catch this fish."

She closed her mouth.

A tic in the back of his elevated arm caught her eye and she flinched at the clear sign that he was fighting fatigue. "Look, Zack," she whispered. "We have enough to eat. We don't need fi—"

An explosion of movement erupted, so sudden and powerful, Olivia was momentarily paralyzed. An instant later, Zack sat up. His arm outstretched, a silvery entrée flapped in his fist. "Gotcha!" he said, through clenched teeth.

Olivia blinked with surprise and pushed up to sit. "You did it!" she cried. "You actually caught a fish with your bare hands!" Exhilarated, she flung her arms around his neck. "Amazing!"

Her delight wasn't brought on by the knowledge that she would soon be eating, but by a deep, primitive female appreciation for this supreme male animal and his mastery over what she'd thought was a barren environment. The bounty he'd conjured up out of practically nothing was astounding. As far as she was concerned, Zachary Merit held a well-earned monopoly on courage and virility.

"I'll never forget this moment, not as long as I live," she cried. Overwhelmed, she kissed his cheek. His day-old beard scratched pleasantly against her mouth, but the stirring sensation also told her in no uncertain terms that she'd actually kissed the man. *Again!*

Aghast, she pulled away.

His quick, troubled glance cut off her breath. "Why did you have to come over here?" he growled.

Before she could respond, his lips came down hard on hers, full of passion and anger.

CHAPTER NINE

HIS kiss was rough, aggressive, holding her hostage, stealing her breath. Nothing could have prepared her for the sexual electricity of his lips as they brutally possessed hers. Stunned and helpless, she quivered, fire spreading through her limbs. Using his free arm, Zack drew her against him, a groan issuing up from deep in his chest.

She clung to him, an unspeakable desire overtaking her. Angry or gentle, his kiss was unlike any experience she'd ever known, and she knew in her heart of hearts Zachary Merit's kisses were what she'd waited for all her life. His powerful, male hardness pressed against her thigh and she gasped with anticipation and delight. Now! He would make love to her *now*! Out here under the sun, in the full, naked brightness of day, all wild and willing abandon, and it would be glorious.

Hugging him close, she offered him everything of herself with sweet spontaneity, every curve of her body softly molding to him.

Suddenly, quite out of place, she heard a guttural growl, grating, disorienting. The next instant, his kiss ended as abruptly as it had begun. "*Damn it*, Liv," he muttered, his voice raw and husky. "This is not going to happen." He turned away. "You need food, not sex. Go—get the rinse water."

Dazed and light-headed, she slowly drew her arms from around him. Her body still tingled with the hot, hard feel of his warm flesh. Somewhere inside, from the depths of her soul, she heard a grief-stricken wail of re-

121

jection and loss. With it came a rending pain, the like of which she'd never known.

Bewildered and crazily furious, she tried to focus on his profile, her emotions raw. "Why did you do that?"

"Sunstroke." He thrust a hand through his hair. "Just go."

"Right." She pushed up on wobbly legs. "Rinse water." Unable to help herself, she glared at him. "That last lesson was—" Her voice broke and she couldn't go on.

His jaw working, he shoved up to stand. "Give me the knife and I'll clean the fish."

He held out his hand. Olivia made sure to keep her attention fixed on his palm while she fumbled in her pocket. When she handed him the knife she was dismayed to see how badly her fingers shook.

She didn't know how much time passed or quite what happened after that, because she couldn't think straight. At some point, she realized Zack was steaming the first batch of limpets over hot stones covered with seaweed. What surprised her the most was she'd actually eaten several sea urchin gonads and a fistful of seaweed.

She slowly began to come back to some semblance of reality. Emotionally numb, she made a point to concentrate on the food. It was better than thinking about Zachary's punishing kiss.

Listless and miserable, she huddled on a tuft of sea grass. Beside her Zack had spread out the linen napkin that accompanied her long-ago consumed peanut butter sandwich. He transferred the steamed limpets to the makeshift platter.

She absently noticed the fish, blackening and sizzling above the fire. It had been speared onto the sharpened end of a green stick, the other end buried in sand to secure it at the correct angle for cooking.

"Eat."

Zachary's command made her jump. Avoiding eye contact, she picked at the mollusks, finally slipping one into her mouth. She had to admit it tasted a little like escargot. Sniffing the air she got her first whiff of roasting fish. It smelled heavenly, which surprised her, since she'd never been a big fish fan.

Movement caught her attention and she turned to see Zack operate on one of the remaining spiny sea urchins as he nimbly extracted the edible light brown roe. He held it toward her.

"What?"

"My guess would be you eat it," he said.

The explosive kiss was obviously still preying heavily on his mind, too. His expression was grim, his voice tight.

She lifted her chin in a pitifully unconvincing act of defiance. He gave her a "don't argue" look, so she plucked it from his fingers and ate it. "Happy?"

He watched her narrowly. "How do you like it?"

She swallowed. "Fine." She'd be darned if she'd praise his culinary talents, now! All she wanted to do was curl up in a ball and cry. But that would never do. She had *some* pride!

In all honesty, the food wasn't bad and would have been really good with a little seasoning. No matter how unhappy she was, she had to admit Zack's gourmet feast of Haunted Rock cuisine had been an amazing feat.

She inhaled the brine-tinged air. A breeze fluffed her hair, and she had the oddest surge of contentment. She liked the island, and the sunshine, the scent of the fire and the sizzling fish. It would be perfect if only...

She glanced at Zack. Unable to help herself, she surveyed him, though she knew it was a dumb thing to do. Admiring his competence in this natural, primitive setting wouldn't do her any good. She needed to be reminded of his *incompetent* side.

Wordlessly Zack handed her another sea urchin gonad, which she took without argument. Chewing it, she frowned. Exactly what incompetent side did Zack have? Where had she seen him when he'd been less than perfect?

Dragging her gaze away, she tried to concentrate on the surf and the flight of a seagull as it plummeted and soared and shrieked.

She heard movement and shifted to see Zack tug the fish's stake out of the sand and lay the cooked carcass on the napkin. "Don't worry about the blackened skin. The meat will be fine and flaky."

He sat back and crossed his long legs at the ankles. His hair was dry, and his jeans were nearly so, which was both a curse and a blessing. Though she tried not to make him a major concern, she couldn't help noticing he hadn't reached for any of the food. He merely sat and looked out to sea. It was painfully clear he was avoiding eye contact with her. Well, that was just peachy! She didn't crave having him watch her with that brooding expression, anyway.

Her thoughts scurried on their own back to his kiss. Why had he done it? She absently leaned over to blow on the fish to cool it. What lesson had he been teaching? To beware of what you ask for because you might get it? Or to let her know she was playing with fire and that he was more than able to burn?

Her face blazed at the memory. He'd held her with one arm, giving every impression that he was losing control just as thoroughly as she was. But he hadn't lost control at all! He'd remained *so* controlled, he'd managed to hold onto a slippery fish the entire time! *How insulting could he be?* And the kiss—erotically angry as it was—had lasted scant seconds. If his brief, scornful kiss could do her so much damage, then what would his lovemaking do? What kind of havoc would that wreak? A sob welled in her throat and she choked it down.

Maybe the lesson had been a blessing. Maybe she'd had to be shown just how antagonistic his feelings for her were—show her in no uncertain terms how awkward her continued unwarranted attacks could make a person feel. Awkward was too mild a word. Oh, it might be the right word for him, but as for her, the right word was devastating.

Long, drawn-out minutes dragged by as she sat in silence, trying to pretend she was alone. Even so, every fiber of her being seemed intent upon reminding her that he was only three feet away, the breeze playing in his hair. After a tension-filled eternity, Olivia couldn't help but ask, "Aren't you hungry?"

He glanced her way. The noontime sun caused the long fringe of his eyelashes to cast shadows on his cheeks. She'd never seen such a sexy phenomenon in her life and she was fearful she wouldn't soon forget it. After a moment of contemplating her question, he shrugged, the move more stimulating than it had any right to be. "You eat. You're the one who's on sick leave."

She pulled up her knees and hugged them, his cool attitude chilling her. "Don't be silly. There's plenty of food."

He indicated the napkin. "I caught that fish for you, now eat it."

She lay her chin on her knees and frowned at him.

"Don't be stubborn. I'm not eating another bite until you eat something." She picked up a seaweed frond. "Here. It's pretty good. Tastes like sweet asparagus."

"I know," he muttered, glancing out to sea. "I said, I'm not hungry."

She had no idea what alien urge possessed her, but she couldn't help scooping up a limpet and scrambling over beside him. She was mad and restless and suddenly very determined. "Don't act like a child, Zachary. You need to eat, too. I insist."

He frowned at the morsel, then her. "You heard what I said."

"You're not the boss of me." She came up on her knees. "Eat this or I will take that nice, flaky fish you worked so hard to catch and throw it in the sea."

He presented her with a "be very careful" frown. "The first rule of survival is, don't waste food."

She canted her head. "Exactly. So eat the stupid limpet."

Pursing his lips, he returned his gaze to the ocean. "Look, I'm not in the mood for games."

She made a quick decision. "Zack?"

He flicked a glance her way. "Wh—"

As soon as he started to speak she stuffed the mollusk between his lips. *"Swallow!"* She slapped her hand over his mouth. "You're going to eat if I have to force-feed you like a two year old!"

She shoved with all her might, pushing him down. When he was flat on his back, she planted both hands over his mouth. "For days you've made my life miserable in your backhanded pretense at helping me come out of my shell. Well, you must be doing something right, because even if I have to die for it, you *will* eat!"

"Mmmff."

She giggled, not sure why. Maybe it was the tickle of his protest on the palm of her hand. Maybe it was the surge of power she felt, straddling his belly. Maybe it was her sense of freedom out here on this pile of sand and rocks, some primitive life force flowing from the sea and the sun and the wind, or radiating up from the earth, causing this uncharacteristic deluge of spontaneity and enthusiasm.

Maybe it had something to do with his admonishing kiss. Quite possibly it had driven her a little insane. She didn't know, didn't care. She liked this feeling and planned to flow with it, see where it led. "Or are you a big faker?" she taunted. "Don't you have the *guts* to eat poor man's escargot and raw gonads?"

He grasped her wrists and she knew she wouldn't be in control much longer. "Zack, wait!" she cried, a vain attempt to get him to listen to reason. Sadly, from everything Olivia knew about human nature, any person attacked as he had been wasn't normally of a mind to lie calmly on the sand and listen to his attacker's version of reason. Detecting a glitter of intent in his eyes, she gulped down a nervous breath. "Zack—*don't be hasty!*"

He jerked her hands off his face. Her support taken away, she fell flat on top of him.

"Oof!"

Before she could orient herself, the world toppled and spun. When she opened her eyes, she stared up at his massive silhouette, back-lit by bright, blue sky. Her arms were splayed out on the sand, his fingers entwined with hers. Though he straddled her, he put no weight on her, hovering just out of reach. "Are you up for feeding me any more limpets, Miss Nordstrom?" he asked, unsmiling, yet not quite frowning. He just stared, his eyes daring her.

She stared back for a pulse-pounding moment, mes-merized by the deliriously sexual vision he made poised above her. That is, in less antagonistic circumstances, she *might* have thought that. At it was, she was his captive, not his lover. He'd made his opinion on that subject all too clear. She eyed him with determination, unsure where the foolhardy surge of defiance came from. "Did you eat it?"

His prominent cheekbones and dark lashes accentuated narrowed eyes. A fallen wave of ebony hair drooped over his forehead, lending him a dangerous quality, empha-sized when he clenched his jaws and his cheek muscles bunched. "Not before I nearly inhaled it."

She felt a tug of regret about her recklessness. She could have caused him to choke. Her defiance fading a bit, she broke eye contact. "Well—that's what you get for being so stubborn."

He didn't respond, and she grew uneasy with the silent standoff. She squirmed, then regretted her unintentional bump and grind. And that wasn't her only regret. The sand on her neck and arms clawed unmercifully. "Ouch!" She bit her lip, angry with herself for showing weakness.

"What's wrong?" Though he looked perturbed, his eyes showed a tinge of concern.

"Nothing." She winced, and looked away. Why did the sand feel like needles piercing her flesh?

He didn't say anything for what seemed like forever. Olivia tried to gather her poise by watching the surf hiss ashore and rove along the beach, but it didn't work. She would give anything to take back the rash act that brought her to this.

The position they were in was far too symbolic, and the irony stung. "Zack—let me go," she whispered.

She chanced a peek at his face. His expression had gone from perturbed to rueful. "Hell—" he muttered, "you're burned to a crisp."

"Well, well" came a masculine voice from some distance away. "Am I interrupting?"

Zack recognized the amused skepticism in Jake's tone, and ground out an oath. If his luck didn't change, he might as well face the fact that Jake would never let him hear the end of this little wrestling match. He looked up, scowling at his brother, who was ambling toward them. "What's the matter?" Zack called. "Did all the search and rescue dogs die?"

Casting Olivia a concerned look, he let go of one hand and shifted to her side. "I'll help you up."

Her expression was bleak but she didn't say no, so he tugged her to her feet. By the time Jake reached them, they'd dusted off most of the sand.

"Hi, you two," Jake said, grinning. "I see being stranded on an island hasn't hampered your inner children."

Zack kicked sand on the smoldering fire. "Could we put off the monologue. Olivia needs first aid." He felt like a jerk for not paying more attention. Since she was a brunette, he'd assumed...*hell*, what did it matter. He was wrong. He'd been so caught up in keeping his eyes and his mind off her, he'd been negligent.

Jake let out a low whistle as he examined Olivia's back. Guilt-ridden Zack did a slow survey, too. She stood stiffly, as though she had on a cloak of cactus spines. Her sweater's scooped neck, short sleeves and bare midriff revealed quite a bit of skin, all free to burn at its leisure. Which it had. Plus, she'd rolled up her pant legs. The tops of her feet and the backs of her calves were bright red. Poor kid. She was in for some uncomfortable hours.

"Good Lord, Zack," Jake said, incredulous. "With a burn like this, you were rolling her in sand?"

"I wasn't rolling her in—"

"It wasn't Zack's fault," Olivia cut in. "I attacked him."

Jake looked at her. "You?"

With a wave and a wince, she indicated the scattering of food on the linen. "I decided to feed him." Gingerly she plucked at the back of her sweater. "The stubborn fool wouldn't eat."

"Let's do the postmortem later," Zack cut in. "You need to get that burn seen to."

As they trudged to the boat, Jake walked beside Olivia, always the caring host. Zack lagged behind, grabbing the bedroll and miscellany. He was angry with himself. Not only for allowing Olivia to get a bad sunburn, but for what he'd wanted to do back there in the sand. Hell— the insane kiss had been bad enough. But obviously, considering what he'd *almost* done just now, he was a slow learner.

It was pure providential intervention that Jake showed up at the precise second he did. *Damn it, man!* he charged inwardly. *When you hauled off and kissed her back there, you forgot for a minute, she's here on a time-out until she's restored herself enough to return to her button-down world. You are not supposed to make love to her— or damage her.*

At least this fiasco had taught him one thing. No more of this search-for-Liv's-wild-side foolishness. What if she'd been really hurt, or drowned? No matter how hard he tried not to, he cared about her. If she didn't have this "loosening up" bug out of her system yet, then she would have to find some other idiot to pester about it, because as of this minute, he was through.

"Say, Bro? Did you hear me?"

Zack looked up. "What?"

"I said, have you seen any of the planes?"

Zack was confused. "What planes?"

They rounded the bend and Zack could see the Merit security cruiser moored near the smaller disabled vessel. Men in gray scrambled around their boat. It looked like they'd deduced the trouble and were installing new batteries. One thing you could say about Jake, he was competent. Dependable. One solid citizen. Things Zack never seemed to be able to be. Neither Jake nor Marc would have allowed Olivia to get so burned. He ground his teeth with self-disgust.

"Paparazzi."

Zack had lost the thread of the conversation and frowned. "What?"

Jake and Olivia stood at the water's edge. Jake shifted to look back as Zack approached, but Olivia stared at the boats. Zack had a feeling the reason had less to do with her fascination about what was going on than to avoid looking at him. He couldn't blame her. Trying to get his mind on track, he shook his head to clear it. "What about paparazzi?"

"They found out where you and Olivia are. Planes and helicopters have been buzzing the island all morning. Boats packed with reporters are everywhere. I'm surprised you haven't seen any."

He winked, and Zack received the message loud and clear. Jake was saying, *"If what I saw between you and Liv was any indication, you were too well occupied to notice anything but each other."*

Zack tramped forward and unceremoniously dumped

the supplies and bedroll in his brother's arms. "Here," he grumbled. "Merry Christmas."

"How do you think they found out?" Olivia asked Jake, still ignoring Zack. "This is awful. It'll fuel the engagement stories!"

"Who's fault is that?" Zack scooped her up in his arms and waded into the water.

"Oh!" She instinctively grabbed him, then seemed to realize who she was grabbing and let go. Pressing against his chest, she demanded, "What are you doing? Put me down!"

"The salt water would sting your burn." He kept his eyes on the boat's ladder and his mind off the fact that he'd just done another rash thing. "Your sunburn is my fault."

"Are you suggesting the paparazzi showing up is *my* fault?"

A helicopter appeared from behind the rocky hill and swooped down. A man with a high-powered camera hung out the side. As the chopper hovered like a fat, unwelcome horsefly, the shutterbug snapped away.

"I didn't say it was your fault," Zack yelled over the noise of the copter's rotor blades.

"But you're thinking it!"

Zack reached the ladder. "Grab on."

She didn't turn or move, just glared. "If you would care to hear my theory—it could have been your *date* who blabbed. She might not have liked being stood up."

"She didn't have a date with both of us. And *you're* the photo op." Zack nodded toward the ladder. "They've had their quota, now get aboard."

"You think somebody in Daddy's office leaked it?"

The likelihood had crossed his mind. When he didn't immediately deny the possibility, she looked incensed.

"No one in my father's confidence would stoop so low for free publicity."

"Maybe it's not free publicity they're after. Maybe it's a spy for the other side, and they're after dirt."

"What?"

He had no idea why he was standing in hip-deep water with Olivia Nordstrom in his arms, having a discussion on dirty politics. It was too freakish to dwell on. "Your father's the Guardian-Of-Family-Morals candidate. Maybe somebody's trying to catch his squeaky clean daughter and—" Zack paused, then decided he might as well spit it out "—and a notorious fast-living bad boy in something kinky."

His suggestion sent a flash of shock across her features, but she quickly regained herself. "Oh, *really*?" She peered up at the helicopter as it buzzed into the distance. "Then, isn't it a shame we didn't get pictures of what happened last night!" Grabbing the ladder, she lurched from his arms. Before Zack could register what she said, she'd disappeared over the gunwale.

"Or this morning," he muttered.

A deep chuckle right behind Zack made him cringe.

"So, little brother…" Jake queried, "just what *did* happen last night—and this morning?"

Zack squeezed his eyes shut and counted to ten.

CHAPTER TEN

OLIVIA peered at herself in the mirror. Yesterday's outing in the sun tinted her face an ironically healthy color. The color of her nose was a tad healthier than the rest of her face, but not so much that she looked like Rudolph the Red Nosed Reindeer. Whatever had been in the salve Marc gave her for sunburn had worked miracles. She didn't think she would even peel.

That was about the only positive thing she could come up with for what had happened out there on Haunted Rock.

She wasn't going to peel.

Making a face at her reflection, Olivia recalled this morning's telephone call from Jerry Skelton. Apparently that picture of Zack carrying her in his arms had made it into newspapers nationwide, after Jerry had made it "abundantly clear" to reporters that she and Zachary were *not* engaged.

Jerry complained that the offensive picture had made a jackass and a boob out of him, when it had been accompanied by the headline Are They Or Aren't They? He'd sternly added that her father was livid, seeing her "carousing with a notorious ne'er-do-well" when she was *supposed* to be getting good nutrition and rest.

Olivia didn't have an excuse for either her father or for Jerry, though she didn't owe the campaign manager any excuses. She couldn't be held responsible for statements he made that might come back and bite him. Just because Jerry thought she would one day become his fiancée didn't give him any right to tell her how to spend her time.

"Why didn't you tell him that, ninny?" she muttered at her reflection. *Because,* a small voice inside her head jeered, *you're not sure that one day you won't become engaged to him. He's a bright, aggressive mover and shaker, very likely to become one of the most influential men in D.C. You and Jerry would make an enviable duo among Washington's political elite. For that matter, one day Jerry might even be president.* "You could do a lot of good as his wife," she mumbled. "Your life would be fast-paced and possibly even historically significant."

Absently she picked up a brush from the dressertop and ran it through her hair. After a dozen jerky strokes, while she eyed her reflection morosely, the world went blurry. She blinked back tears. *"Get your mind off Zack!"*

Struggling for a hold on her emotions, she slammed down the brush. It was time to quit her whining and go in search of Mimi, Susan and the babies. They always lifted her spirits.

Most days after lunch the women lounged on the shady loggia and played with the babies until naptime. Marc would be making rounds in his cruiser today. Jake was either supervising at the mine or working in his office, and George would be taking his afternoon siesta.

The single unknown quantity was Zack. Heaven knew where he might be. She couldn't guess. The only thing she could do was pray he'd opted to go deep-sea diving or was busy lecturing the miners on parachute folding and limpet steaming. Anything that would keep them far enough apart to hinder her urges to run into his arms.

True, he made her furious half the time, but most of her fury came from the fact that he could ignore her so thoroughly she could almost go up in flames before he noticed.

Antsy and disconcerted at the recollection of yesterday on Haunted Rock, she checked herself in the mirror one more time. Little Benjamin had spit up on her blouse after his noon bottle, so she'd changed into this cropped, cotton T-shirt. A strip of pink tummy peeked out above her beige shorts. She'd grow accustomed to seeing her midsection, so it didn't startle her any longer. Other than that slice of belly, she didn't look a bit wild today.

Fighting a wave of dejection, she spun from the mirror. Even if Zack hadn't told her in no uncertain terms his participation in her wildness search was over, their night on Haunted Rock had thoroughly dampened her enthusiasm for the quest. Had there been any wildness in her soul, she'd have handled Zack's rejection in an entirely different way. She'd have teased him and toyed with him until she'd turned him on so completely that...that...

She shook her head. But she hadn't. She was a left-brained paper pusher with a geeky talent for numbers, not a temptress who could laugh in the face of setbacks and turn a rejection into conquest. Zack had been right to scoff. If anybody could recognize a wild woman—or, in her case, the complete opposite of one—it was Zachary Merit.

When she stepped out onto the loggia, her expectant smile froze. Zachary paced along the stone floor, a squalling baby in his arms. He pivoted to retrace his steps and spotted her before she could sneak inside. Though he hesitated a half step, he merely nodded and continued to pace, patting Benjamin's back and murmuring to him.

The baby continued to bellow, his pudgy face beet-red. Olivia scanned the expanse of the shaded patio. Nobody else was there. "What's going on?" she asked, loud enough to be heard.

"Ben's not happy."

"No kidding." She walked over to Zack and he came to a halt, but continued to pat the infant's back. "Where is everybody?" she asked.

"Mimi wasn't feeling well. A little afternoon-morning-sickness, so she went to lie down. Kyle fell asleep. Susan took him inside for his nap."

Olivia had never seen Zachary hold one of the children. She hadn't even thought he would consider it. "Would you like me to call one of the maids?"

He gently swayed with the baby, patting and cooing. When she asked the question, he frowned. "Why? Do you think watching a maid vacuum the patio would make Ben happy?"

She fought a grin brought on by much more than Zack's dry wit. He looked cute cuddling Benjamin. He didn't look one hundred percent comfortable, but he didn't look overwhelmed, either. "Would you like me to take him?"

"You?" His expression grew skeptical. "Since when do you know anything about babies?"

"I don't know much, but I bet I know as much as you." She held out her arms. "Have you checked to see if he's wet?"

"He's not. He just needs to burp."

Right on cue, Ben let out a foghorn belch so deafening it startled the crying right out of him. His wide-eyed little face looked comically astounded, as his head wobbled disjointedly in his search for the source of the big noise.

Olivia giggled. "When you're right, you're right." As soon as she heard her words, she was struck by the irony.

He'd been right about more than just Ben's need to burp.
Her amusement faded.

"Would you like me to take him?" she asked, wondering why she didn't simply leave. Hadn't she hoped
against hope she wouldn't run into him? Why was she
lingering? On the other hand, as soon as he relinquished
Ben to her care, he'd be free to go. No doubt he had
plans for the afternoon. Having someone take over baby-
sitting chores would give him an excuse to make his get-
away.

Besides, she reasoned, sitting on the loggia cuddling
Ben would help calm her frayed nerves. All in all, having
her take the baby was the best solution for both of them.
She stretched out her arms.

Instead of handing over the baby, he surprised her by
ambling away. "No, thanks. Ben and I have things to
do."

Confused, she watched him carry Ben off the loggia
onto the lawn. An expansive rose garden lay not far
away, with meandering stone pathways, statuary and
fountains. The day was overcast, so the paparazzi fly-
overs had dropped to a trickle. Boats full of nosy media
bobbed in the distance, though Merit Island security kept
them from coming too close.

Olivia walked to the edge of the patio and leaned
against a stone pillar. "Where are you taking Ben?"

Without looking back, he called, "Man stuff."

He angled away from the garden and headed toward
the back of the mansion. "Man stuff?" she murmured,
her curiosity giving her fits. First, she'd been floored to
discover Zachary would even pick up a baby. To think
he'd go off someplace with Benjamin didn't even com-
pute. What could a macho-man like Zack do with a tiny
infant? She'd never suspected he might have a nurturing

side. But then, she'd never suspected he could catch fish with his bare hands, or that he could kiss like some Greek Kissing God—

She made a pained face, banishing the erotic memories.

He disappeared over a rise, heading toward the woods behind the house. Olivia pushed away from the wall and stretched on tiptoe to try to see farther. It did no good. He was gone. She knew following him was the worst thing she could do, so she made herself pivot in the opposite direction. After a lot of mindless wandering along stone pathways amid the haven of blossoming roses, she happened upon a marble bench and sat down. Contemplating the beauty of Merit Island's exquisite gardens had to be a sure way to calm her nerves.

Particularly striking silver-hued blossoms reached toward the bench. Olivia cupped a large bloom and sniffed. Soft sweetness filled her senses. If there had been any chance at all that this exercise in ignoring Zachary would work, this sojourn in the garden would do it.

It didn't.

Olivia glanced at her watch. Twenty minutes had passed since Zack carried Benjamin into the forest. Irked with herself for what she was about to do, she jumped up from the bench and marched out of the garden. Trotting across the lawn, she aimed for the woodland that enveloped the island's interior.

"Curiosity killed the cat," she mumbled, but the insight did no good. She was dying to crack this riddle of where Zachary and Baby Ben had gone. *Or is it really that you can't stand the idea of not being around Zachary? Wouldn't you be out looking for him whether Benjamin was with him or not?*

"No!" She yanked down on the short hem of her top.

"And— *Oh, quit talking to yourself. You're turning into a babbling idiot!*"

She trudged toward the trees, though a part of her demanded she turn back. When she was less than a car's length from the edge of the wood, movement caught her eye and she sensed Zachary was nearby.

Her heart going to her throat, she struggled to keep her breathing normal. This was a ridiculous way to behave over a man who found her company annoying at best.

He strolled out of the woodland, his hands plunged in his pockets, his expression grimly contemplative. He must have been deep in thought, because he was about to pass by her without registering she was there.

Typical, she thought. *He can't even see me when I'm right in front of him.*

Well, that was perfect! She didn't want to chat with him, anyway. She would take Benjamin off his hands, then she and the darling child would have a good—

Her head snapped up and she spun to stare at Zack. With a gasp, she cried, *"Where's Benjamin?"*

Zack blinked and turned, obviously startled to see her.

"Zack!" She turned on him. *"What have you done!"*

He stared at her, and even the air seemed to hold its breath. His square jaw tensed and some strange emotion crossed his face, something she could only describe as a chilling shock. An unfamiliar coldness invaded his eyes. Or did it? Almost instantly, his lips twisted in a crooked grin.

"I see your opinion of me remains intact," he said. "Thanks. But to answer your question..." He cocked his head toward the woods. "I left Ben with his father—as requested." A dark eyebrow rose in mocking query. "Is there anything else I can ease your mind about?" His tone held sardonic weariness. "Would it quiet your fears to know how many maidens I *didn't* ravage while skulking in the underbrush?''

Olivia felt sick about her rash, unfair assumption. What had possessed her? Guilt and regret lodged in her chest like twin millstones. "Oh—Zack, I'm so—''

"*Don't* bother!'' He jerked up a halting hand. "Forget it.'' For one debilitating instant their gazes clashed, then he turned and walked away.

Olivia stared after him; a heavy, sodden dullness around her heart made it difficult to catch her breath.

Zack paid scant attention to his dinner. This afternoon's scene by the forest's edge kept running through his head. He'd have to have the IQ of a turnip not to see Olivia thought of him as such a reckless maniac he would mislay his own infant nephew.

He cut a bite of steak, watching her covertly, across the table between his brothers. She burst out laughing at one of Jake's stories, and Zack felt the impact of the soft, sexy sound deep in his gut. Naturally she'd be impressed by Jake, find him entertaining. He was a respected businessman, CEO of a multimillion dollar emerald empire. Jake would be completely acceptable in Olivia's circle of friends.

His glance slid to Marc, on Olivia's right. The good doctor. Healer. Saver of lives. Solid, respectable Dr. Merit. Comparing himself with his responsible, successful brothers brought him to a painful awareness. He didn't measure up. His differences with his father all those years ago, his intensely independent nature and his need to get out from under the old man's dictates, had cost him much more than decades of estrangement from his family. Years of reckless wandering, trifling in anything exciting that involved speed, had turned him into the edgy misfit he was today.

Before he set foot on Merit Island two weeks ago, he'd already identified his need to find a real life and shake off his black sheep ways. But until this afternoon when he'd seen Olivia's shocked expression, he hadn't fully grasped the enormity of his flaws.

He didn't hold out any foolish notion that making a change would alter her opinion of him. Yet, if it could at least banish the memory of the horror in her eyes when—

Zack felt a hand take his wrist, the light touch drawing him from his musings. He shifted, puzzled, to look at Susan's smiling face.

She lifted her hand from his arm, indicating George, at the head of the dining-room table. "Your father asked you a question, but you were a thousand miles away."

Mystified, Zack glanced at George. The old man hadn't spoken ten civil words to him since their bitter confrontation. Anticipating the usual condemnation, he forced a pleasant grin. "Sorry, Dad. What did you say?"

George cleared his throat importantly, and Zack braced for what was to come. "I simply commented that you ate the eggplant casserole."

Zack hadn't expected anything as ordinary and conversational as that. He glanced at his plate then back at his father. "It was good."

George's eyebrows knit for a beat, then his expression cleared. "As a boy, you hated eggplant."

Zack grinned. "As a boy, I hated a lot of things. But I grew up—eventually."

George seemed to contemplate that statement, then nodded. "Yes…well…" He broke eye contact with Zack and patted his lips with his napkin. After another throat clearing he directed his attention to Mimi, sitting at his left hand. "Are you feeling better this evening, my dear?"

Mimi responded, but Zack's attention remained on George. He experienced an odd sensation in his chest. Was it the birth of hope—that this was perhaps the beginning of the end of a lifetime of yearning that one day he and his father could get along, without bellowing or blaming or belittling? Was it too much to ask, or even dream?

His gaze drifted to Olivia, and their eyes met. The effect was like a lightning strike, painful and electrifying. The impact lasted only a flash before her glance skidded sideways toward Marc, when he took the conversational reins.

A maid came in and whispered to Jake.

Nodding, he stood. "Excuse me a second." Ten minutes later, he strode back into the dining room, his expression vaguely perturbed. "We have a visitor."

Just then, noise at the arched entryway told Zack someone else had stalked inside, and he turned.

A tall, trim man appeared, wearing an expensive, three-piece charcoal suit and yellow power tie. He looked like an upper-echelon mobster type, with a square wall of a forehead and a black moustache that might have been drawn on by a felt-tip pen. His hair was jet-black and slicked back. A superior sneer rode fleshy lips. Zack didn't know why, but he took an instant dislike to the stranger.

His opinion didn't improve when, without acknowledging anyone in the room, the newcomer made a beeline for Olivia. He clasped his hands on her shoulders and stooped to kiss her cheek. "This place is harder to get into than Fort Knox,'' he grumbled, then peered at her more closely. "Livy, what happened to your face?"

Olivia touched her cheek, then seemed to understand. "Oh—sunburn. It's fine."

He frowned. "You poor thing. I'm glad I insisted on coming." Straightening, he scanned those assembled until he spied Zack. "You're our skydiving friend." He continued to massage Olivia's shoulders as his remark echoed in Zack's head.

"Well, really, young man!" George bellowed, his complexion ruddy with outrage. "By what right do you burst—"

"That's okay, Dad," Zack cut in. "I think I know." Soberly he observed the stranger whose hands were all over Olivia. No one had spoken to Zack in such a condescending tone since he'd been fourteen when he'd corrected a tyrannical teacher. Rather than acceding he'd been wrong, the schoolmaster had snapped, "So, you think you're smarter than I am, Mr. Merit? Then why don't you take over the class!" Red-faced, the old bully had marched out of the classroom. Zack didn't like arrogant smart-asses then and he hadn't mellowed on the subject. "Yes, I'm the sky diver," he said, quirking an affable smile. "And I gather you're Olivia's masseur?"

The man's eyebrows shot up, as though he'd been pricked in the backside. "*I'm* Jerry Skelton, Senator Nordstrom's campaign manager."

Zack suspected as much, but didn't let on. "Oh?" Lounging back he indicated the seated family members. "Well, Jerry, in case you're curious, we're the Merits. George, my father, is on the end. These lovely ladies on either side of me are Susan and Mimi, my sisters-in-law. The gentlemen to your right and left are my brothers, Jake and Marc. Won't you join us for dinner?"

"Yes, Jerry." Olivia touched his hand on her shoulder. Her expression was pleasant, though vaguely pained. "Do sit down." She shifted to look at him. "Actually, you're hurting me."

"What?"

She touched his hand again. "Sunburn, remember?"

"Oh, right." He moved his hands, but didn't relinquish his touch. His fingers lightly clasped her upper arms. The proprietary act cut like ground glass in Zachary's belly.

"What are you doing here?" Olivia asked.

"You've been gone for over a week now." He leaned down to smile at her. His tolerant expression grating. "We need you at headquarters, Livy." He squeezed her gently, glancing at Zack, then back at Olivia. "We must get this ridiculous engagement thing cleared up. Besides, did you forget you're scheduled to be on CNN's *Talk Back Live* on Wednesday? That's the day after tomorrow."

She closed her eyes for a second. "Already?" With a resigned sigh she nodded. "Right." Glancing at Zack, she added, "We do need to work out some statement."

"Never fear." Jerry straightened, passing Zack a belligerent stare. "I've had one typed up. All our friend here has to do is sign."

Zack was annoyed with Skelton's cocksure, buddy-boy attitude. "Thanks, Jer." He folded his arms across his chest. "But, I'll have to look at it. I wouldn't want some poorly worded document giving the public the wrong idea of my relationship with the senator's daughter."

"*Poorly worded!* I'll have you know—"

"Uh…yes, Jerry," Olivia cut in, casting Zack a look that seemed to mix an apology with a reproach. "We'll go over it all this evening…together. Just to make sure it states everything correctly." She smiled shyly. "After all, I've caused the Merits quite a bit of bother. I want to make sure the announcement suits Zachary. It's the least I can do."

"But, Livy…" Jerry rubbed his hands along her arms. "I'd planned for us to catch the red-eye out tonight."

"Oh, Mr. Skelton, we insist you extend your visit for at least a day," Susan broke in with a gracious smile. "We rarely have such eminent visitors. Naturally we're interested in hearing Senator Nordstrom's plans for the country. A substantial contribution isn't out of the question…" She paused, and Zack could almost see dollar signs form in Jerry's eyes as he calculated the vastness of the Merit fortune and how it could benefit their campaign war chest. "We'd be heartbroken if we didn't get to spend some time with you. Wouldn't we, sweetheart?"

"Absolutely," Jake said, a twitch of mirth hovering around his mouth. Zack didn't know why his family would put themselves through this, and he wasn't sure he wanted them to. At least not for him. As far as he was concerned the sooner Olivia was out of his life, the sooner he could start working on forgetting her.

Possibly Susan's affection for Olivia had spurred her to issue the invitation. The idea of cutting short Liv's visit so abruptly had been insensitive of the campaign manager. Zack had a sneaking suspicion "insensitivity" was the jerk's middle name.

With a wave toward a maid standing at the ready, Jake said, "Josephine, set a place for Mr. Skelton."

Minutes later, Jerry was seated beside Marc. A plate of food set cooling before him as he expounded on the economical, social and moral imperatives why Senator Nordstrom must be elected the next President of the United States.

As Jerry droned on, Zack found his attention drawn to Olivia more than he cared to admit. She sat forward watching Skelton, seeming to soak up every long-winded, tedious word. Even considering her sunburn, she looked overly flushed. Zack wondered if the added color was due to excitement at the surprise visit from her boyfriend. He didn't want to dwell on it, so why in Hades did his brain seem unable to dwell on anything else?

CHAPTER ELEVEN

OLIVIA pulled her pillow from beneath her head and crushed it over her face. Dawn crept through the curtains—her last dawn on Merit Island. She didn't want to see the sunrise. She didn't want to say goodbye to the Merit family.

Especially not Zachary.

Beneath her downy shield, she thought about him. Inhaling the freshly laundered scent of fine cotton, she conjured up his face—his hawkish features, well-formed mouth, sexy dimples and emerald eyes. She even loved the little scar on his chin.

Groaning, she gripped handfuls of pillow. It made no difference that she could successfully block out the sunrise. No matter how hard she tried, she would never wash Zachary Merit from memory. Whether she left the island today, tomorrow or next week, it wouldn't make any difference. Zachary's image would linger in her mind and heart.

His demeanor last night haunted her. After dinner, she, Zack and Jerry had gone over the statement for the press. Actually, "gone over" was an exaggeration. Zack didn't even sit down. When Jerry handed the typed letter to him, he'd scanned it, his expression unreadable. Before Olivia could seat herself and cross her legs, he tossed the page to the coffee table saying it looked "great, just great." Then he'd strode off. That had been her last glimpse of Zack.

The rest of the evening went by in a haze of half-recollections. Susan, Jake, Marc and Mimi had acted the perfect hosts and hostesses as Jerry held court. George hadn't even tried to mask his dislike of their guest, and hustled his grandchildren off to the nursery for "story time."

Zack simply disappeared. She knew she shouldn't be surprised. She had no right to be upset. Zack was a guest on the island, too, and far from the methodical kind of man his brothers were. He couldn't be predicted or restrained. He was like lightning, magical yet shattering.

Her conscious mind had skipped and skidded along the evening's discourse, her heart pining over a loss she was a fool even to conceive. She moaned, the sound muffled in her ears. "I can't leave like this!"

Good Lord, Zachary had saved her life, and what had she done for him? Lots and lots—all bad! She'd made him miserable with a media-drenched movie that would probably never have been made if she hadn't been Senator Nordstrom's daughter. She'd blurted to the press that she and Zachary were *engaged*, forcing him to run for cover clear across the country. She'd wasted his time indulging her in her absurd loosening up project. Worst of all, yesterday she'd insulted him, virtually accusing him of dumping his nephew in the woods.

All in all, he'd been through a ton of grief on her account. Definitely more than his share. Just because she'd managed to get her heart tangled in the rigging of his charisma, didn't give her leave to walk away without a backward glance. It might be easier—considering what being near him did to her insides—but it was the coward's way. Before they returned to their separate worlds, she owed Zack a moment alone to express the depth of her gratitude, no matter how unbearably sad it would be to bid him a last goodbye.

"*Enough* self-pity," she grumbled. Pitching the pillow aside, she looked toward the window. The sky had grown lighter, the heavens blushing a fluorescent pink. Jumping out of bed, she yanked off her nightgown. In two minutes she'd thrown on deck shoes, jeans and a knit top that matched the vivid, morning sky. Finger-combing her hair, she dashed next door to Zack's room. Without giving herself time to come up with all the reasons this was a bad idea, she knocked. "Zack?" she called in a semi-whisper. "Are you up?"

Nothing happened. No response, no sounds of life. She frowned, wondering if he'd taken the opportunity to make up for missing his date while stranded on Haunted Rock. Had he gone into Portland in search of a good time? Her belly constricted. Would he simply take off to carouse? Did he plan to be gone until after she left? *Why not?* an imp in her brain scoffed. *What or who could stop him?* She closed her eyes, utterly miserable. Zack hadn't invited her to the island, so he wasn't responsible for seeing her off. It was as simple as that.

"Zack?" She knocked again, recoiling at the panicky edge to her voice. Composing herself, she said, "I need to talk to you. Are you in there?"

Tense and fidgety, she waited, listening to the sound of her own shallow breathing. Nothing, not a creak of bedsprings nor the faint thud of a foot hitting carpet, gave her hope Zack was on the other side of that door.

Positive he was gone, she pressed the flats of her hands against the wood and lolled her forehead on the cool surface. "Darn you, Zack," she said. "Why must you be so—so *undependable*?"

Heaving a despondent exhale, she shoved away. As she took a step toward her room, she heard a click, then the telltale squeak of a door opening. Startled, she jerked toward the sound.

Zachary stood there, cover-model cuddly, wearing nothing but a pair of low-slung black boxers. His dark hair was mussed in a stroke-me-you-fool come-on. His eyelids hovered at half-mast. She couldn't tell if he was groggy from being awakened, or guarded. She prayed he hadn't heard her complaint through the door.

He slouched against the jamb, flashing a wry grin. "Thanks. I won't have to give blood this year."

Olivia detected the awful truth behind his show of teeth. He'd had about enough of her abuse. What was her problem? Why was she always hurting the man, when she thought the world of him?

She sensed coiled tension in him, but when he crossed his arms over his chest, the easy fluidity of muscle gave no hint of stress. "What can I do for you?" he asked. "Or did you just want one last dig for the road?"

Olivia winced. Clearing her throat, she shook her head. "No—I—" She shook her head again, trying to focus. *What do you want, Olivia?* In all honesty, she knew what she wanted, but that was out of the question. Zack could hardly abide the sight of her, let alone...

So, what could she *tell* him she wanted? A thought struck, and she grabbed on for dear life. "I—I'd be forever grateful if you'd take me for a boat ride before I leave." She smiled, but from the stiff way her lips felt, she knew the effort was flawed. "I'd—I'd like to go really fast. Feel the ocean spray on my face."

Yes, that was perfect. She'd get him out on a boat— in his element. He'd be more at ease and she'd have the time to tell him how indebted she was that he'd saved her life. And since then, for his patient endurance about the dratted movie and the engagement fiasco. Most importantly, she wanted to tell him she was grateful for his—friendship. She *hoped* she could leave Merit Island with that, at least.

He frowned. "You want to go on a boat ride, now?"

"If it wouldn't be too much trouble," she whispered. "Jerry and I have to leave at nine."

He stared at her, as though trying to see into her brain. "What about the paparazzi?"

She hadn't thought of that—wasn't thinking clearly. "They don't start congregating for another hour," she said, relieved she could think at all. "We'd have time if we hurry."

He seemed to consider it, but his knitted brow made it obvious that taking her on a boat ride wasn't high on his list of things he was dying to do.

Sensing he needed a push, she lifted her chin and made direct eye contact. "Please?" She flinched. That pitiful whine was hardly a tap. He merely continued to stare and scowl. Despairing, she spread her arms wide. "I promise, it's the *last* favor I'll ever ask of you."

The emerald brilliance of his eyes flared for an instant, as though she'd struck a nerve. After a slight pause, his lips crooked. "How can I refuse such a generous offer?" He took a step back. "Give me a second."

The door closed between them and Olivia's foolish heart boomed in the quiet. She concentrated on taking deep breaths to steady her nerves and force her pulse rate to a less lethal pace.

A minute later he reappeared, startling her when he tossed a flannel shirt at her and planted a soft-brimmed hat on her head. "Put on the shirt and tuck your hair under the hat." When she looked up at him, he thrust a pair of sunglasses on her face. "There will be a few paparazzi out early. I'd rather they think we're fisher-men."

Though the world had taken on a dark cast, she could see him. He wore a long-sleeve navy shirt, worn jeans and a red baseball cap, the brim pulled low over his brow. With a jerk of his head, he indicated the flannel dangling from her hand. "Get it on, Miss Nordstrom, or forget the boat ride."

She realized her mouth was open, so she closed it. Swallowing, she shrugged into the soft flannel.

"Come on."

She fumbled to fasten the shirt as he towed her down the hallway.

"What's your hurry?" she asked, trying to keep pace and button up at the same time. "Do you have an early date in Portland?" Where had *that* question come from? Appalled, she made a face.

At the head of the stairs he slowed his breakneck advance, but only slightly. "I thought you wanted to avoid as much of the press as possible."

"I do." She jammed her hair up inside the hat. "But I don't think we'll look much like buddies out for a lazy day of fishing if you're dragging me across the lawn on my face." She grabbed her floppy hat brim and yanked it down over her ears. Her sunglasses were so big, they barely rode the tip of her nose.

Zack eyed her for an instant, and Olivia thought she saw the reluctant twitch of amusement on his lips. Too quickly, he turned away to open the front door.

Was he smirking at her? She wanted him to smile at her, not smirk! Not mock! After all, the stupid disguise was his idea! "I hope you're not laughing at me!" she said, then immediately wished she hadn't blurted that aloud.

"Hope away, sweetheart." He hauled her toward the dock, gesturing in the direction of boat slips. "The family doesn't own any racing boats, but that second one from the end is a sport fishing boat. It'll have to do."

"Whatever." She wondered if he would lighten up enough to give her a chance to be open with him. *Drat you, Olivia*, she chided. *You make the chance! Stop quivering like a jellyfish and grow a backbone! If you're going to thank him properly and sincerely, it has to be soon!*

Zack aimed her toward the fishing boat, which didn't look much different from any other cabin cruiser. Maybe there was a little more scaffolding-looking stuff on top, but otherwise it was just another cruiser to her. They boarded, and Zack led her to the fly bridge. Moments later the sleek craft was slicing through choppy Atlantic waves.

Without a word or sideways glance, Zack piloted them away from the island. Several tense, uncommunicative minutes plodded by as Olivia mentally worked on her speech. She became aware Zack was revving the engine to full speed.

She grabbed the shiny brass railing, exhilaration sweeping over her. The sheer power Zack commanded was thrilling, her delight increasing with their momentum. The craft skimmed along the surface like the king of seabirds. Ocean spray misted her face and she licked salt from her lips.

She had a flash of realization. How could she live in California and never have felt salt spray in her face? How could she have allowed herself to be so stifled? This wild hare was such a kick, such a liberating joy, she laughed out loud.

No wonder Zack loved racing boats. While they hurdled along, they were set free from the world, soaring, out of reach of the mundane. Whooping with delight, she grinned at him. Their gazes clashed and she realized he'd been watching her. Though his features were shadowed by the cap's brim, she had the sense he felt grudging gratification at her pleasure.

Now, she thought. *Tell him now!* "Zack, I—"

"It's going to get rough," he broke in, pointing ahead. "It's shallow up ahead. You can see a couple of places where rock breaks the surface."

He turned the boat. Immediately Olivia noticed a change in the texture of their jaunt. The cruiser began to *thud, thud, thud* across the corrugated sea in a bone-jarring staccato. She was stunned and dismayed at how hostile a slight turn into the wind would feel in her knees and stomach. It didn't take long for her to start feeling queasy.

Finally they skimmed safely by the rocks. "Uh—can we go the other direction, now?" She had to shout the question, which was hard, since rising nausea made it imperative she keep her mouth closed at all cost.

This was a rotten turn of events. How could she thank Zack if she was hanging over the side, hoping to die?

She felt Zack's gaze. Gulping down bile, she peeked at him.

"Are you seasick?" he asked.

She must have looked as green as she felt. Cupping a hand over her mouth, she nodded.

His jaw muscles bunched. "Sorry." Turning the wheel, he maneuvered them to a less nauseating course. Even so, Olivia was afraid her exhilaration over the outing had been nipped back badly.

"Is that better?"

She nodded, but didn't take her hand away from her mouth.

''Look at the horizon. That'll help.''

She did as he suggested. Along with the horizon, she saw a few boats headed toward them. The media circus was coming to work. She pointed, but didn't want to chance speaking.

''I see them.'' He looked at her. ''Do you want to go back?''

She hesitated. That wasn't what she wanted to want, darn it. But she felt terrible. Besides, once the press showed up in force, they'd have to turn back, anyway. She nodded, but there was nothing enthusiastic about it.

He gave a curt answering nod. ''Whatever the lady wants.'' Altering course, he added, ''It'll be rougher going back.''

She groaned, cursing herself. Why couldn't she take a simple boat ride without turning into a squeamish baby? No wonder Zack had no respect for her. She didn't deserve respect.

Inwardly she berated herself while deciding which needed holding more, her mouth or her stomach. Though her mind was divided, she began to notice something interrupting her intentness on the horizon. Whatever it was, it was growing. She swallowed several times, trying to get her mind off being sick and figuring out what the thing was.

A plane, she decided. A single engine plane. It darted toward them at a fast clip. Without warning it dived directly at them. Olivia only had time to gasp as it blitzed by, low and close. From the elevated platform where they stood, she could actually look *down* into the plane's cockpit.

''*Zack!*''

''Hell!'' He pushed the boat into a tight turn.

The sudden change in direction made her pitch toward

the rail. In a horrifying instant, she pictured herself falling overboard, and screamed. At the last second, she was snatched in a sheltering embrace. Though jolted, she didn't go over the side.

Flabbergasted, she realized she wasn't even hurt. A low groan came from somewhere behind her, then the safeguarding arms wrapped about her went slack. A second later Zack crumpled to the deck.

In a state of shock, Olivia stared down at him. Her mind had trouble computing such an unlikely event— Zachary Merit, strong, capable, heroic, lying so still, so— "Zack?" She knelt beside him, too late comprehending he'd taken the full force of the blow to save her.

"Oh—*my Lord*!" she cried. "Zack!" She touched his face, but he didn't register the contact. It was then she noticed blood pooling beneath his head. "Oh—God, *please...*"

Scrambling to her knees, she grabbed the rail to steady herself as she stood. Somewhere in the back of her mind she noted she was no longer wearing the sunglasses. Doubtless, they resided in the deep blue sea by now. Without Zack's intervention, she would be down there, too.

The boat skipped over the waves at a breakneck pace. Even shaken and panicky, Olivia knew she'd have to slow their speed. They couldn't dock going this fast. It would kill them both.

Thankfully the boat had righted itself and now sped in a straight line. Olivia peered over the bow and her heart rocketed to her throat. A murderous wall of granite loomed above the pounding waves.

Straight ahead.

"Don't panic," she muttered. "You saw Zack drive this thing." She scanned the controls. Sending up a prayer, she tentatively took the wheel and began to turn it. As she did, she grasped the throttle lever and pulled in an attempt to reduce their speed. She didn't know how long she held her breath, but she felt faint by the time she was sure they would miss the rocks—by inches.

She inhaled and cast a glance at Zack. He lifted a shoulder as though trying to get up. "Don't move," she shouted. "Let me—I'll be right there."

He opened his eyes, but only for a second. His eyebrows knit in a wince of pain.

"Just lie there." She searched the horizon, trying to determine which way Merit Island was. "Let's see, the sun was on our right." She closed her eyes to concentrate. "Yes…" She scanned the sky. "So—so it would need to be on our left…" She maneuvered the sports fisher in the direction she hoped was right.

Her stomach churned with fear and nausea. She clamped her jaws together, commanding, *Damn you, Olivia! You will not be sick! You will get Zack help! Then you can pass out!*

The same, obnoxious airplane made another pass, but thankfully didn't come close enough to jeopardize the boat. Olivia couldn't believe their gall. Surely they knew they'd almost caused a tragedy—*maybe had caused one, if Zack's injury was as bad as it looked.*

She shook her fist in the air, not caring if her picture did end up plastered on tabloids across the country. She only wished she could get the idiots up there within eye-blacking distance.

She cast a worried look at Zachary. He was trying to rise up on one elbow.

"No…" She relinquished the controls and rushed to grab a nearby life vest. Hurrying to kneel beside him she tossed the vest down and coaxed him to lie back, with the vest elevating his head. "Stay still." She tugged off her flannel shirt and pressed it against the ugly gash above his right ear. "Just—just lie there and press this on the ga—er, thing."

He watched her, his expression squinty. She didn't know if it was from pain or because the sun was in his eyes. "Just—just don't move." Torn, she drew up on her knees. She wanted to stay with him, comfort him, but she had to drive the dratted boat.

She scrambled up and faced the wheel. Off in the distance, she saw a misty shape that hadn't been there before. "Oh—please…" she mouthed, hoping against hope Merit Island rose before her out of the sea.

Not many minutes later, her hopes were confirmed when she saw a familiar Merit security cruiser and waved. She wished she knew how to use the radio, but Zack hadn't used it. Determination bolstering her courage, she clamped her jaws. She was nearly home. She only had to get the boat up to the wharf. It might not be the smoothest docking in the world, but she could do it.

Zack groaned.

She flicked her attention to him, worry gnawing at her. "Just another few minutes," she called, hoping he could understand. "We're almost home."

He frowned, his eyelids fluttering. "Home?"

She watched the word form on his lips, but couldn't hear it. "Yes—home." A melancholy tug in her breast brought tears to her eyes and she blinked them back. Of course he would be confused. This wasn't his home. It wasn't hers. They were both visitors here, and they would soon be gone—to separate worlds, separate lives.

"I didn't know—you could pilot a boat," he said, sounding woozy.

His eyes opened and he frowned up at her.

Me, either, she said to herself. "Don't talk," she called, returning her attention to her driving.

"I'm okay."

She passed him a doubtful look. "You're bleeding like Niagara Falls."

He lifted the flannel away from his wound. The shirt was a ghastly mess. He gave it a curious glance. "Head wounds—bleed. It's nothing..."

"Well, your head is my responsibility right now. So lie still and shut up until Marc sees you."

With one eye closed, he watched her for a couple of pulse beats, then gave a small nod of resignation. "Whatever—the lady wants."

She made a disgruntled face, but felt a surge of hope. Zack seemed rational, if not one hundred percent clearheaded. Still, they weren't out of the woods. She had to dock the boat.

Lucky for her, there were only two cruisers moored there, giving her a good expanse of open dock to aim for. Sucking in a shaky breath, she aimed the bow and slowed the engine to a crawl. When she saw one of the security crew approach along the lawn, she honked and frantically waved to get him to come running.

When he did, she shouted. "Zack's hurt! Get Marc!" The uniformed man stilled for an instant, as though he wasn't sure he'd heard right, but she motioned with both hands that he go. "*Run!* He's bleeding!"

The man spoke a couple of words into a shoulder apparatus, then took off.

As they neared the dock, Olivia faced the fact they were on a collision course and would hit even without the help of the engines. She turned off the ignition, and the rumble died. Seconds later, the bow struck rubber bumpers attached to the pier. The collision knocked her back a step, but she decided it could have been much worse.

She didn't have any idea how to get Zachary to Marc, but her quandary didn't last long. The guard's alert had been heard, and in seconds the boat swarmed with Merit personnel. Even so, Olivia didn't take a calm breath until Marc climbed aboard. Zachary's eyes were closed, again, and she had a sinking feeling he'd lapsed into unconsciousness.

She held his hand for reassurance—for his, and hers. Marc made a quick survey of Zack's wound and she quickly explained how the accident happened. When two guards arrived with a stretcher, she rose to get out of the way, but was startled when Zack's grip held her captive. Marc's attention was drawn to Zachary's unconscious propriety. "Maybe you'd better stay," he said. "Can you deal with the sight of blood?"

She nodded, counseling inwardly. *Zachary needs you to be strong, Olivia! You do not have permission to faint!*

"Oh—*son!*"

Olivia blinked at the torment in George's tone. The old man clambered awkwardly aboard, elbowing aside a burly security guard. "Let me pass, you moron! He's my boy!"

When George fell to his knees alongside Marc, he grasped Zack's free hand in both of his. "Oh, son…" His voice croaked with emotion. "I've been a stubborn fool. I've tried—tried to find a way to say I'm sorry…" His eyes watery, his features pale and haggard, he turned on Marc. "He'll be all right! He must!"

Marc was busy swathing Zack's head in a temporary bandage. "I have to get him to my office, Dad. He needs stitches, and he could have a concussion." After taping down the gauze, Marc faced his father, touching the old man's knobby hands as they clutched Zachary's fingers. "He'll be okay, Dad. I—promise."

A chill raced along Olivia's spine at Marc's slight hesitation. *Zack would be all right! He had to be!* She scanned Zachary's face, his head bound in white gauze. Even with his golden California tan, he looked pale. Red began to stain the sterile wrap, and she had to fight to keep from pulling him to her breast, sobbing out her pain, her guilt and her crazy, foolish love.

Marc motioned toward the stretcher bearers. "Okay, men. Get him to my office."

Olivia was forced to peel Zack's fingers from hers so he could be lowered over the side. She wanted to go with him, but with George hovering and all that needed to be done, she would only be in the way. Besides she wasn't family, and in an hour she was leaving.

Leaving. The word had a desolate sound. Yet she had no choice. There was nothing—no one—for her here. Besides, she had a job to do. An important job.

Long after the procession carrying Zack away had disappeared over a rise, Olivia stood alone on the lawn, staring after it. Strong, invincible Zack, handsome heartthrob and hero, laid low. And why? Because, once again, he'd tempted fate to save her life.

"Congratulations," she mumbled, swiping at a tear. "On top of everything else, you almost *killed* him."

CHAPTER TWELVE

OLIVIA and Jerry left the Merit mansion with only a but-
ler to bid them farewell. Olivia hadn't expected to end
her stay with Zachary's family in such a detached, barren
way, but she understood. The family had gathered at the
doctor's quarters out of concern for Zachary's condition.
Olivia was concerned, too. The last thing she wanted to
do was rush off to catch a plane.

Jerry carried her borrowed suitcase in one hand while
he clutched her elbow in the other. She didn't like the
feeling of being pushed, and she felt very pushed as Jerry
outlined her upcoming schedule and how it coordinated
with her father's. Typical of Jerry, he was oblivious to
her troubled state of mind. He always assumed she felt
the same way about everything as he did. She heaved a
sigh, the long weeks and months of late-night strategy
meetings and living on stale coffee stared her in the face.

That was depressing enough, but she'd barely had time
to hug Susan and Jake goodbye. She'd caught them on
the run, as they'd hurried to Marc's cottage office. She
hadn't seen Mimi at all. Olivia knew the whole clan was
down there, being supportive—being a family. A heaviness centered in her chest. She wished she were there,
too.

As Jerry talked, leading her along the lawn, she had a
sudden need to make sure Zachary was okay. *It was the
least she could do.* She came to an abrupt halt, yanking
Jerry to a stop. He quit talking in midinstruction and

glanced at her, obviously clueless. "What are you doing?" he asked.

She pointed to the stone cottage down the slope, off to their left. "I'm going to check on Zachary."

"Why? They're doing everything they can. He'll be fine."

Olivia had no intention of arguing about it and pulled from his grip. "You go on to the cruiser. Tell them I'll be there in five minutes."

"But, Livy—"

"Five minutes," she broke in. "The longer you insist on debating this, Jerry, the longer it'll take."

He lifted his free hand as though in surrender, but he looked annoyed. "Okay, okay. No need to bite my head off." He cast a perturbed glance at the stone cottage. "Just hurry."

"Make that *ten* minutes." She spun away, her thoughts veering to Zachary. Jerry and his stopwatch mentality moved to a back shelf in her mind as she ran toward the cottage. One of her high heels sank into the turf and she almost stumbled. "Dratted useless shoes!" she muttered, pulling them off.

"What are you doing now?"

She looked back, surprised that Jerry hadn't moved. He stood in the same spot, gaping at her. She threw a shoe in his direction and he caught it. "You take care of these." She tossed the other one, and he had to duck to avoid being hit between the eyes.

"Hey! Watch it!"

She couldn't restrain an irreverent grin. "Oops."

"Livy, you'll ruin your stockings!"

She waved him off. "Don't be an old poop."

She dashed toward the cabin. Her heart pounded with a mixture of hope that Zack was better and dread that he wasn't. She cried under her breath, "Please, *please*, let him be sitting up, joking with his brothers. Even if he's furious with me, I don't care. *Just let him be all right.*"

She didn't bother to knock at the cottage door. She knew this was not only Marc and Mimi's residence, but also Marc's office. On alternate weekdays, when he wasn't visiting the bedridden and sickly on neighboring islands, he saw patients here. She went inside and closed the door. Scanning those milling in the rustic-country room, her immediate impression was one of expectancy. Of waiting. Even the patients seemed concerned. When the door banged shut, all eyes turned toward her.

The Merit family had congregated around the leather couch. George sat stiffly, looking worried. Susan was a cushion away, petting Foo Foo, Marc and Mimi's poodle, curled in her lap. Jake had settled on the sofa arm, his hand on his wife's shoulder.

"Why, Liv." Mimi stood beside the sofa, pausing in the act of pouring coffee in George's mug. "We thought you'd gone."

"I—I couldn't go until I found out how Zachary's doing."

George lay his mug on the side table and pushed himself up from his seat. Though his expression was sober, she sensed less anxiety in the set of his mouth.

"It was good of you to come, my dear." He crossed the room and took both her hands. "Zachary is conscious now. Marc is just finishing stitching up his head." He walked with her toward a door. "I know you must catch a plane, so I'm sure Marc won't mind if you say your goodbyes. Especially since you so bravely brought the boat back."

Olivia didn't think she'd ever seen George this talkative, at least not to anyone but his precious grandbabies.

She wondered if Zachary's brush with disaster had been a wake-up call for the older man, forcing him to see how quickly those we love could be taken away from us. She hoped so, not only for Zachary's sake, but for George's.

The elder Merit turned the knob and poked his head inside. "Marc, might Zachary receive a visitor? Liv must go soon, and she wanted to—"

"Come in."

Olivia was surprised to hear Zack's voice rather than Marc's. He sounded hoarse, but the fact that he was conscious and talking sent a wave of relief through her.

George touched her between her shoulder blades, coaxing her forward. "Go in, my dear. And thank you for— everything."

She glanced at her companion, astonished by the glisten of emotion in his eyes. Unable to force words past the lump in her throat, she squeezed his hand, then pushed through the door.

The room was all white and gleaming stainless steel, a typical doctor's examining room. The atypical sight was Zachary. Long, lean and gorgeous, he lazed on the examining table. She wondered if medical periodicals peddled office equipment with pictures like this—a hunky male model sprawled on the merchandise, provocatively eyeing the camera. If they didn't, they should, considering how many female doctors bought equipment, too.

She closed the door, watching as he turned to his side and rose up on one elbow. Dark hair fell across a white, gauze bandage swathing his forehead. One of his eyebrows was covered by the dressing. That eye was black, his cheek puffy and bruised. But to Olivia, he looked absolutely flawless.

"Are you okay?" he asked, surveying her with a concerned expression.

Marc and his male nurse stepped away, seeming to understand the duo needed a moment alone.

She moved to Zack's side. When she heard the click of a closing door, she knew they were alone. Inhaling for strength, she shook her head at him. "Am *I* okay?" She indicated his trussed-up head. "You look like an escapee from that movie, *The Mummy*, and you ask if *I'm* okay?"

He winced. "Don't mention movies to me."

His plagued tone made her cheeks burn with rekindled guilt. "Sorry." She touched him. She didn't mean to, but some part of her couldn't help it. Deciding it would be too humiliating to yank her hand away as though she'd been scalded, she pretended touching him was merely a charitable inclination to urge him to lie down. "Relax. Don't strain yourself on my account." Prudently she removed her hand from his shoulder and backed a step away. "How are you feeling?"

He lay flat and looked up at her. His gaze steady but questioning. Good heavens, even looking out at her amid all that purple, damaged flesh, those eyes were cruelly mesmerizing. He looked terribly vulnerable, and she knew he was hurting. She had to fight the urge to take him in her arms. Clasping her hands together, she resolved not to make a big, stupid fool of herself, again.

"I'm fine." His lips crooked in a lazy grin. "I do this to get women."

She smiled, surprised by his joke, but her nose tickled with a need to burst into tears. "It'll never work," she lied. "You look horrible."

He flashed his teeth. "Women love helpless men."

"You? Helpless?" she said, trying to match his light mood. "That'll be the day."

Father Time was swiftly devouring her ten minutes. She felt every pulse-throbbing second as it slid away, and she sobered. "I—I'm glad you're better," she said, reaching out to smooth back a lock of hair. At the last second she recognized her insanity and stopped herself, motioning toward his wound. "That was my fault," she said. "I apologize for that, and for all the other troubles I've caused you." She swallowed to steady her voice. "I was going to say—I mean while we were out on the boat, I wanted to ask..." She blinked, fighting tears.

"What?" From his guarded expression, Olivia could tell he thought she was going to ask another favor, like would he mind jumping off a roof for one parting bout of amusement. She didn't blame him for being dubious, and fiddled with a button on her linen jacket. "I was hoping—we could part as—friends." The word sounded so antiseptic, considering how she really felt, what she really wanted. But she was a math geek and he was a speed demon. She'd completely failed to gain entry into his world and he had no interest in hers.

The woman who could eventually tame him would be fortunate, but as for her, it was time to return to her world. Zack was a fantasy man. Every woman had one tucked away in some secret corner of her heart.

Now, so did she.

"I wouldn't like to leave—thinking you hate me," she finished lamely.

He closed his eyes, and Olivia experienced a rush of panic. "Zack? Are you okay?"

She saw his jaw muscles clench. When he looked at her again, his smile was wry. "Don't panic, sweetheart. I've got the hardest head in the family. It's documented." His glance slid to the utilitarian steel-and-white clock that hung beside the stainless cabinets. "You'd better go or you'll miss your flight." He lifted a hand. "Friend."

There he lay, sporting heaven knew how many stitches, done up in yards of gauze. His head probably throbbed unmercifully and he'd lost a lot of blood, all due to her. He could have rejected her bid for friendship. He had every right. He could even have yelled at her and called her an idiot for daring to ask. Yet, he'd lifted his hand in a gesture of goodwill.

Her heart swelled. She appreciated his generosity more than she could express. She appreciated it so much that a mere handshake was not worthy of their last goodbye. She took his hand between both of hers and squeezed his fingers in a wordless show of gratitude. Without allowing herself to dwell on why, she bent and kissed his lips. The rash intimacy was slight and quickly over, but it meant the world to her. "Thank you, Zack," she whispered.

A moment later she rushed out of the cottage, toward the dock, silently threatening herself with all kinds of grief if she shed *one* single tear.

Zack was so surprised when Olivia kissed him, it took several seconds for him to register that it had happened. Obviously his brain wasn't functioning at full capacity. *Damn it*, he didn't want her to leave! Even her barely there kiss affected him more than a sweaty romp with some lusty, pouty-lipped nymphet. He was insane, he knew, but he was in love with Olivia Nordstrom, and he couldn't just let her walk casually out of his life!

He pushed off the examining table and headed for the door. A couple of strides buckled his knees and he went down hard. Pain shot up his legs and exploded in his head. Biting back a groan, he shoved up to stand. The world pitched sideways, then went black.

CHAPTER THIRTEEN

"YOU crazy man." Marc clasped Zack's shoulder in a gesture of affection. "I told you you'd lost too much blood. What were you doing—trying to walk?"

Zack opened his eyes to find himself lying on Marc's sofa. His family was gathered around, looking worried. "Crazy man" was fitting, he decided. He'd definitely lost his reason when he stumbled after Olivia.

Had he forgotten who she was? Who he was? *The princess and the dropout. Yep, Merit old buddy, you're a lucky bastard you conked out. It saved you from getting laughed at in your face.*

"How do you feel?" Mimi asked, stroking his cheek. Her pretty brow knit and he experienced a rush of self-reproach for putting his family through this. He winked, then winced. *Not with that eye, stupid!* "I'm great," he said, the hoarseness in his voice proving the statement a lie.

Mimi's smile was less than reassured. "Marc says you need to stay off your feet for a while, build your strength. He just pumped every spare milliliter of A-positive blood out of Jake to bring you back to us, sweetie. You lie still while I rustle you up a bowl of my award-winning leek soup."

She kissed his forehead and left. Zack noticed several miners had closed in on the sofa, too. Patients, no doubt. He looked for Marc, then realized he'd gone on with his doctoring. Jake stood at the foot of the sofa, his arm around Susan. George hovered nearby, appearing gray and gaunt.

"Look, everybody," he said. "I'm fine, really." Struggling to a sitting position, he shook his head to get focused. With a great force of will, he made his legs lift him to stand, damning himself to the lowest level of hell if *anything* in his expression or stance gave away his weakness. The last thing he intended to be was an object of pity.

"Thanks for the blood, big brother." With a quick grin at Jake, he indicated the back of the house. "Why don't I buy you lunch. If I don't miss my guess, the food's in the kitchen, and I'm starved." He took a step. Though he felt woozy, he refused to give in to it.

Before he could take a second step, he felt hands grip his arm and was startled to find his father had come to his aid.

"Let me help, son." Though George didn't smile, Zack sensed a corner had been turned in their relationship. Finally he'd been forgiven. That knowledge opened a new reservoir of strength deep inside him. At that instant, both his new wound, and a very old one, began to heal.

Zack grappled with an urge to punch a fist through Marc's kitchen wall. Troubled and edgy, he needed to get back to living his life. In the fourteen days since Liv had gone back to California, the movie that caused them so much grief was taking a back seat to the latest summer blockbuster. Soon the celluloid drama he and Liv shared would be forgotten. And as far as the senator's daughter was concerned, so would he.

Zack knew the drill. Society princesses might crave a week or two of excitement but they settled down with

Mr. Solid. And damn him, he'd been ready, willing and able to give them their taste of hedonistic pleasure for more years than he cared to admit.

"I wonder if there's a support group for ex-studs?" he muttered. That part of his life was over. From the first time Liv smiled at him, he'd known having a wild sexual spree with her, just to watch her walk away, would be too hard on him. Maybe he'd finally grown up, for once using his *brain* to do his thinking instead of his—er—

A rush of annoyance washed over him and he rattled his newspaper, trying to concentrate on the words. "Finally you showed a *little* strength of character, Merit," he mumbled under his breath.

From the newspaper photos he'd seen over the past two weeks, it seemed clear Liv would eventually marry Slick Jerry. They were always photographed arm in arm at some gala or reception. So what if *he* thought Skelton was an insolent jerk. It wasn't his business who Liv did or didn't marry. Who she did or didn't love. Zack might as well face the fact he'd become an unfocused memory to Liv, a part of her past.

He flipped the page, spreading the paper out on the kitchen table as he waited for a gap in Marc's appointments. It was "Stitches Removal Day." Mimi was in Portland for one of her environmental causes, so he was alone in the little kitchen, except for Foo Foo, curled between his feet.

"Damn," he mumbled. "I have to make some changes in my life. But what?" What was he trained for? What was he good at, except driving things fast? And how could a talent like that lead to a fulfilling life?

He'd already informed his speedboat racing partners he was through. He'd lost his taste for competition. If he were brutally honest, he'd lost his taste for everything he'd been for the past twenty years. He wanted to do something worthwhile. Something he could look back on one day and say, "I did that."

"What the hell am I good for?"

"You've been doing a lot of that lately."

Zack stiffened, turning at the sound of Marc's voice. "A lot of what?"

"Muttering to yourself." Marc stripped off a pair of surgical gloves and tossed them in a covered trash container. "What's grinding in your gut?" He went to the kitchen sink and lathered his hands, peering at his brother. "You can tell me, I'm a doctor."

Zack grinned wryly. "Thanks, but I think I'll take a pass."

"Okay, but I'm very wise." Marc's expression was comically deadpan as he toweled his hands. "You're missing a great opportunity to solve all your problems."

Zack laughed at his brother's kidding, relieved to note he could laugh at all. "If I was in the habit of making good decisions, I'd be in the U.S. Senate by now." Zack flinched. *The Senate? Why did I say the Senate, of all things?*

"Oh?" With a light touch on Zack's temple, Marc checked the stitches. "I never knew you had political aspirations." He angled Zack's head to get a better look at his needlework, then met his brother's gaze. "Or is it the senatorial picnics you're interested in, where the old bureaucrats bring their pretty, grown-up daughters?"

"That's very funny." Zack broke eye contact. "Are you going to remove the stitches or practice your stand-up routine?"

"Don't be so testy. Can't I admire my work for a minute?" He moved a step away. "You're not even going to scar."

"Then I can still enter the Mr. Perfect Hairline contest?"

"Now who's practicing his stand-up routine?" Marc asked.

"Just do it!"

"Okay, okay, Mr. Senator," Marc joked as he retrieved his medical supplies. "Vacations are hard on you, Bro. Why do you suppose that is?"

Zack knew he'd said too much, and opted to keep his mouth shut. He was surprised how quickly and painlessly his brother removed the stitches.

When Marc moved away to dispose of the residue, Zack noticed he'd grown quiet, and seemed engrossed in some sad thought. Zack experienced a guilty twinge. He'd been so wrapped up in his own troubles, he hadn't imagined Marc might have personal millstones weighing him down. "Is Mimi okay?" he asked, concerned. "And the baby?"

Marc stood before the sink, squirting antibacterial soap on his fingertips. He glanced at Zack. "What?"

"Mimi and the baby? Are they okay?" Zack sat forward, resting his forearms on the newspaper. "You look upset."

Marc's eyebrows knit. "Mimi and the baby are perfect, but…"

The pause grew palpable as Marc lathered his hands. He seemed to be reflecting inwardly.

The hair on Zack's nape stood up, and he grew uneasy. Was it George, then? Jake or Susan? One of the children? "*But?*" he prodded, his tone sharper than he'd intended.

Marc seemed to come out of his stupor and turned off the water. Grabbing up the hand-towel, he leaned against the kitchen counter. "I got a letter this morning from a friend who graduated from medical school with me. He had a patient, a little girl, who needed emergency surgery. A tricky operation only a specialist could handle.''

Marc closed his eyes, looking weary. ''She lived on a remote ranch in Wyoming. There was no way to get her to Los Angeles. It was too far and transporting her along with all the medical apparatus cost too much.'' Marc tossed the towel onto the woodblock countertop. ''So, a sweet seven-year-old girl died. Needlessly.'' Marc took the seat opposite Zack at the small table. ''It's damn tough losing any patient, but to lose one just because of distance and money. It's a crime.''

A look of abject sadness passed over Marc's features and Zack felt his brother's pain and frustration. ''So, you're saying if there'd been a plane the little girl might have lived?''

Marc nodded. ''Yeah, but how many families can hire a private plane rigged with medical equipment? It's a nice fantasy.''

''But I've heard of—''

''Oh, sure, Angel Flight and organizations like it are great humanitarian groups, but they can't handle every emergency. Plus, volunteer planes are usually small and unpressurized, so they're not set up for nonambulatory patients in time-critical situations.''

''Hmm.'' Zack scratched his chin, peering at his brother. ''Say—Marc?''

Marc cocked his head, noting the change in Zack's manner. ''Yeah?''

''I fly planes,'' he said, an idea taking root. ''I did commercial runs for a couple of years.''

Marc sat forward. ''No kidding?''

Zack nodded. ''Being an airline pilot bored me, though.''

''Why are you telling me this?''

"I'm thinking it wouldn't be boring if I could help save lives."

Marc's lips quirked. "I've never found it boring."

Zack experienced a wild rush of exhilaration as the inspiration burst full-blown in his head. "Damn it. All I need is a plane."

"That'd be a start."

"But I can't afford one the size I'd need."

Marc shrugged. "With your share of Merit Emeralds, you could."

Zack stared at his brother, confused. "What are you talking about? I was disinherited."

Marc grinned. "So was I. Three times. But we're both pikers compared to Jake. He gets disinherited every year. Old George loves that line, but he doesn't have any more say than…" He looked around, then indicated the poodle that had pitty-patted out from under the table and headed for her food dish. "Than Foo Foo."

Zack frowned, then shook his head. "Well—whatever, I'm not interested in the money."

"No problem. It'll sit there growing until you change your mind."

"I won't."

"And I thought *Jake* was stubborn." Marc relaxed back. "Okay, Mr. Independent, there's always corporate sponsorship."

Zack thought about that. "Right." He was excited, more excited than he'd been about anything in years. This was exactly what he'd been hoping for—a job he could love, one that would be of value. More exhilarated than he'd felt about winning any race, anytime, anywhere, he shoved up from the table. He'd wasted enough of his life sitting around licking his wounds. "I'll start looking for a sponsor right away."

"I'm pretty sure I can guarantee you your first plane, buddy."

Zack stilled. "You can?"

Marc chuckled. "What do you think Merit Emeralds is—a hobby?"

CHAPTER FOURTEEN

Early February

LIV was so exhausted her ears buzzed and she saw double. Pushing hair out of her eyes, she scanned the conference room in her father's California headquarters. The richly paneled walls were all but hidden by stacks of campaign placards, posters, leaflets and donation request mailers. Crumpled pages of cast-off speeches littered the carpet along with discarded electioneering faxes and endless polling data.

Some of her frazzled colleagues sprawled on chairs, while others paced, their energy drawn from gallons of coffee. The Nordstrom camp was well into the primaries. Her dad held the lead, but one misstep, one inappropriate word or rashly answered media charge, and he could be knocked out of the race. American politics had become a minefield, the public weary of tainted leadership.

Today, a candidate had to have lived a moral and ethical life and be in tip-top health. Those who weren't were hunted down by the press and the opposition and bullied or humiliated out of the running. It was stressful and demanding and Olivia was so sick of it she wanted to scream.

She glanced up to see her father stride into the room, deep in conversation with Jerry. She shook her head. Her dad was twice her age and looked robust and full of energy, not like a man who'd been speaking and glad-handing for thirty-six straight hours. His suit didn't show a wrinkle and every strand of his silver hair was in perfect order. He thrived on all this.

On the other hand, she was about to drop in her tracks. "Dad?" she called.

He turned, his concentrated expression softening to one of parental curiosity. "Yes, Olivia?"

She waved an arm at him, wristwatch high. "It's two o'clock in the morning. Can we mortals go home to bed?"

He gave her his infamous "Are You A Quitter?" look. "Do you have those figures I asked for?"

She nodded and sighed. "On your desk."

"What about the latest contribution tally?"

"It won't be available until tomorrow." She stood. "Look, you and Jerry stay and play as long as you like, but the rest of us have got to get some sleep. I picked a fight with the pizza boy this evening. Lucky for you he's sixteen and can't vote this year, but his parents can. I may have lost you two supporters."

The senator frowned. "That's not funny." His dismissive wave showed more disapproval than she would have preferred. "Use the sofa in my private office, if you need a nap. Jerry will wake you at five." His edict given, he clamped his arm around his campaign manager's shoulders and he went back into his executive huddle.

"Gee, thanks, Pop," she mumbled, scooping up her suit jacket. "It'll be really restful, since the phone *never* rings in there!"

She waved to bleary-eyed members of her staff. "You heard, folks. Get some sleep while you can. Meeting at five." No matter how she felt, she tried to look like the proud, workaholic daughter of the future leader of the country. But, she couldn't miss the chorus of groans that trailed her down the hall.

Inside her father's private lair, she slumped against the door. Absently she took in the richly appointed office, brightly lit and cluttered with the day's debris. She flicked off the overhead lighting and kicked her high heels into the shadows. One lamp continued to glow. Fortunately for her debilitated limbs, it was next to the sofa. She padded to it and was about to extinguish the light when something caught her eye.

Yesterday's morning paper lay on the couch, and a grainy picture made her heart skip. Could it be? She sank to the tweedy cushion and tugged the page onto her lap. She didn't have to read the caption to know who it was. She would recognize that marvelous face anywhere. Tears of longing filled her eyes.

Zachary Merit smiled and waved, though it was clear he was heading away from the limelight. A sleek Learjet loomed in the background. Men in white wheeled a stretcher toward a waiting ambulance.

Olivia wiped her eyes to clear her vision and read the caption. "Wings of Merit touched down in Los Angeles today on another miracle pilgrimage by the nonprofit medical emergency foundation. This most recent heroic enterprise took 'Wings' founder, Zachary Merit, and his dedicated crew, on a mercy mission to Argentina, then on to L.A., to help save the life of five-year-old José Galan, suffering from…"

Olivia's tired eyes stung with a flood of new tears. A crazy feeling of abandonment rushed over her. Collapsing back against the couch, she stared, unseeing, at the ceiling.

This wasn't the first time she'd read stories in the national news about Zack and his valiant new undertaking.

But this was the first time he'd flown into Los Angeles. She'd known for months it was only a matter of time before he would. Night after night she'd tried to squelch raging fantasies about it, where he would suddenly appear, here, at her father's headquarters, and without a word, sweep her into his arms and—and...

She choked back a sob. ''But you didn't do that, did you? You didn't even—'' Her voice broke, and she ran a shaky hand over her face. ''Oh, Zack,'' she cried. ''Why couldn't you at least have picked up the phone to say hello?''

CHAPTER FIFTEEN

March

Zack avoided Los Angeles like the plague. The last time he'd flown into town had been a month ago, with little José. It had taken all his willpower not to find Olivia and drag her out of that glittery life she lived. But that would have been selfish, not to mention futile.

Lucky for him an emergency in Anchorage had saved his pride, and more to the point, the life of a two-year-old girl.

But his luck hadn't held and he couldn't avoid this trip. His other three planes and crews were all working emergencies. Well, he could handle being here, again. *It was only one blasted night!* He stretched, bone-weary. He might be tired but his life was good. He was busy and fulfilled—maybe a little lonely, if he let himself think about it.

He ducked into the shower, the hot water working miracles on his tight muscles. The flights were long and most so urgent it was like sitting on a bomb with a short fuse. But the bombs never went off. The people he'd transported survived and thrived. His work was exhilarating and valuable, even if somewhere, deep down, he harbored a vague sadness.

The steamy water felt good. Needing to relax, he forced himself to ignore the fact that he was in L.A., too near the one woman on earth he couldn't get out of his head or his heart.

He stepped from the shower and toweled off, deciding to call home. Mimi's baby was a week overdue and he had a feeling today was the big day. He couldn't believe he was as nervous about the birth as Marc. He'd grown to appreciate time with his family. A year ago who would have bet he and George would be as close as they were now? And it was all due to a parachute that didn't open—and a women he could never have.

Forcing back the memory, he wrapped the towel around his waist and skirted the bed to the end table that held the phone. Dropping to the mattress, he faced the window and looked out over L.A.'s night skyline. He liked California. Maybe he'd set up his new headquarters here. "No," he growled as he dialed. "Steer clear, man. Do you really want to chance running into her with Slick Jerry?"

Marc's number rang. "Hello?"

"Marc? Zack. Do we have a baby?"

Marc chuckled. "Well, I do, old buddy. What you have is a niece. Kelly Marie arrived two hours ago. Six pounds, seven ounces of gorgeous blond."

Zack grinned. "Takes after her mother, then?"

"I love you, too, Bro," Marc said with a chuckle. "How'd the trip go?"

"Great. Surgery's over and little Jenny is doing fine."

"I guess we have a lot to celebrate."

"Sounds like." Zack heard a knock, reminding him he'd ordered room service. "Come in." Without turning, he indicated the dining table beside the door. "Put it there. I've left the tip."

"Are you getting ready to eat?"

"Yeah. Listen, give Mimi and Kelly a kiss for Uncle Zack."

"Will do. And you drop by when you can."

Zack heard a throat being cleared behind him. "I need to sign for the food, Marc. I'll—" He turned around and froze at what he saw.

"Zack? Are you there?"

Frowning in confusion, he remembered he was on the phone. "Uh, yeah…look, I've got to go." Staring at the newcomer, he absently lowered the receiver to the cradle.

"Liv?" He wasn't sure he could trust his eyes. After all these months of struggling to put her out of his head, could she really be there? Sitting on *his* table, dressed in a short black skirt and skinny white sweater? Her legs were crossed and she looked all—beautiful. She held up the bills he'd left for a tip. "You're very generous, Zack. What do you expect me to do for all this?"

Slowly, as though in a trance, he stood and cautiously rounded the bed. The hallucination would end soon. Damn his stubborn, malfunctioning brain! He must be more exhausted than he'd realized.

She looked him up and down, then indicated his attire. "Is that the newest look for you knight-errant types?" She lay the money aside and leaned back on her hands. "I like it."

Perplexed, he looked down at himself, becoming aware that he wore only a towel. But what difference did that make? She was just a figment of his fevered imagination.

The Olivia look-alike phantom recrossed her troublingly lovely legs and he experienced a wrenching pang in his gut.

A flush crept into her cheeks and she cleared her throat. "You know, Zack, you've really thrown Daddy for a loop. Now that you're involved in these altruistic flights, he's having trouble finding you repulsive.''

Zack detected a familiar scent and found himself inhaling greedily. It was *her* essence. Olivia's! He shook his head and ran a hand over his eyes. ''My Lord, it's really…'' he said. ''Liv? What the hell are you doing here?''

''I—I live here.'' Her cheeks fairly glowed, and she seemed nervous. ''I just—when I heard you were back, I thought I'd…'' She cleared her throat, again. ''Did you get a call from Leo last week?''

Zack wasn't doing very well, mentally. Liv was really here. That was mind-boggling enough. He'd been awake for twenty-eight hours straight. His brain couldn't deal with much more. ''Leo?''

''Leo Baskum, head of International Plastics—about his donation of two more planes and crews for Wings of Merit?''

''Oh, yeah. How did you know?''

''I went to school with Julie Baskum, his daughter. You'll be getting a call from the CEO of Intracorp next week.'' Her smile was shy, and her eyes glistened. ''You're doing a wonderful thing, Zack. I want to help.''

He hesitated, blinking in astonishment. ''I don't know what to say.''

''How about, 'You're hired'?''

''Excuse me?'' His sleep-deprived brain was being bombarded by too many conflicting sensations. What was she saying? Where was this heading? The last thing he wanted to do was discuss business. But showing his appreciation by grabbing her and making wild love to her right there on that table seemed a little drastic, even for him.

''It's great of you to help,'' he said. ''I really appreciate your thoughtfulness..." He floundered for something more to say. She'd stated her business, he'd said thank-you. Any second she might go. He didn't want that. "Your dad's ahead in all the polls. Do I need to ask how the campaign's going?"

Liv shrugged. "I think Daddy will struggle along just fine—even though he lost his financial administrator, today."

Zack didn't understand. "I thought that was you."

She broke eye contact. "I quit. I told him I was getting married."

Zack felt like he'd been kicked. "I see." He nodded, numbly. This was the worst news he could imagine, and having Liv tell him was definitely the worst way to get it. "Skelton, right?"

"No. Not Jerry." She pushed off the table and placed the flat of her hands on his chest. Her touch was cold and trembly, but to him it was heaven. He sucked in a startled breath.

"That was a *wild* statement," she whispered, her gaze direct and shimmering. "Since I haven't even heard from you in nearly a year."

Her last sentence didn't make any sense, unless...

He stared. Unless...she was saying she planned to marry *him*. Zack wanted to trust his hearing, but he didn't dare. For months he'd rejected the possibility of marriage to Liv as so outrageous it was unthinkable. The prim princess and the reckless rebel? Such a fantastic daydream didn't have a shot in Hades of—

"Zack?" She slipped her hands up to encircle his neck. "I love you and I'm proposing marriage." Pressing her body against his, she coaxed, "Is that concept too wild for you to deal with?"

Zack experienced a sudden, galvanizing sense of coming home. But he couldn't quite believe his luck. Or should he call it a miracle. The reserve he'd walled himself behind for so long began to crack, and he allowed a cautious grin to quirk his lips. "What about Slick—er—Jerry?"

Liv pressed more intimately against him. "Jerry hates your guts."

"That's a blow," he said, his fatigue-dulled wits beginning to conceive the inconceivable.

Liv didn't smile. "I—I'd like to think you could fit me into your organization—and your life." She lifted up on tiptoe and kissed one corner of his mouth.

The brush of her lips exploded the remainder of his hard-fought restraint. With a provocative stroke of his tongue along her lower lip, he whispered, "I have a feeling you'll be a perfect fit."

"That's reassuring," she said. "But back to my proposal?"

He growled out a guttural chuckle. "For the record, I've loved you since the minute I dragged that parachute canopy off of us and you smiled at me." He lifted her into his arms. "I just never believed..."

"Believe, darling." She kissed him warmly. "And now that we're *really* engaged, would you teach me to be wild?"

"Sweetheart," he murmured, lowering her to the bed. "Welcome to your graduation ceremony."

Passion glowed in her eyes, poignant and awe inspiring. At long last Zachary Merit found the same emotional contentment his brothers had discovered—a worthy role to play in life and the joys of lasting love...with a touch of something wild.

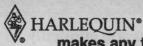

What happens when you suddenly
discover your happy twosome is about
to turn into a...*family?*
Do you laugh?
Do you cry?
Or...do you get married?

The answer is all of the above—and plenty more!

Share the laughter and tears with
Harlequin Romance® as these
unsuspecting couples have to be

When parenthood takes you by surprise!

Authors to look out for include:

**Caroline Anderson—DELIVERED: ONE FAMILY
Barbara McMahon—TEMPORARY FATHER
Grace Green—TWINS INCLUDED!
Liz Fielding—THE BACHELOR'S BABY**

Available wherever Harlequin books are sold.

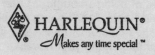